"Welcome to the ranch…"

Wyatt stuck out his hand, and Callie took it.

"If you point me in the right direction, I can get myself moved in." She waved a hand toward the guesthouse.

"Thanks for agreeing to be the manager for the summer. I'll give you a tour of the ranch so you can have a better understanding of what we do. I'll have my daughter with me. I hope that won't be a problem."

"Not at all. She's adorable." She jerked her head toward the yurts. "I'll change into something more appropriate for walking."

Wyatt strode toward the ranch truck, feeling a bit lighter than he did this morning. Talking with Callie had been so easy, just as it had been when they were kids.

If he'd had even a slim desire to date again, Callie was the kind of woman he'd choose. But she was now his employee.

And he wasn't about to do something stupid and risk everything by falling for her…

Heart, home and faith have always been important to **Lisa Jordan**, so writing stories with those elements comes naturally. Happily married for over thirty years to her real-life hero, she and her husband have two grown sons and two rascal rescue dogs. In her free time, Lisa enjoys quality family time, reading and being creative with friends. Learn more about her by visiting www.lisajordanbooks.com.

Books by Lisa Jordan

Love Inspired

Lakeside Reunion
Lakeside Family
Lakeside Sweethearts
Lakeside Redemption
Lakeside Romance
Season of Hope
A Love Redeemed
The Father He Deserves
His Road to Redemption

Stone River Ranch

Rescuing Her Ranch
Redeeming the Cowboy
Bonding with the Cowboy's Daughter

Visit the Author Profile page at LoveInspired.com.

Bonding with the Cowboy's Daughter

LISA JORDAN

LOVE INSPIRED

INSPIRATIONAL ROMANCE

LOVE INSPIRED®
INSPIRATIONAL ROMANCE

Recycling programs for this product may not exist in your area.

ISBN-13: 978-1-335-93144-3

Bonding with the Cowboy's Daughter

Copyright © 2024 by Lisa Jordan

Love Inspired
22 Adelaide St. West, 41st Floor
Toronto, Ontario M5H 4E3, Canada
www.LoveInspired.com

Printed in Lithuania

MIX
Paper | Supporting responsible forestry
FSC® C021394

The Lord is nigh unto them that are of a broken heart; and saveth such as be of a contrite spirit.
—*Psalm* 34:18

Bill and Lynn, it wasn't the year we wanted or even expected, but through it all, God is always good. I'm so glad we faced it together. You're the best siblings on the planet. I love you.

Acknowledgments

Lord, may my words glorify You.

My family—Patrick, Scott and Mitchell. You are the best. I love you forever.

Thank you to Nola Perrin and Nola Santiago of Nola's Angels & Horse Rescue for allowing me to visit and ask so many questions. All mistakes are mine.

Thanks to Jeanne Takenaka, Dana R. Lynn, Christina Miller, Dalyn Weller, Wendy Galinetti, Heidi McCahan, Linda Jo Reed, Kathy Hurst and Susan Anderson for your prayers, brainstorming, encouragement, sprinting and answering so many questions.

Thanks to Cynthia Ruchti, my awesome agent, and Melissa Endlich, my exceptional editor, for your support, grace and patience. And to the Love Inspired team, who works hard to bring my books to print.

Chapter One

What should've been one of the happiest days of her life now brought Callie Morgan nothing but heartache.

Instead of exchanging vows with the man who'd promised to love and cherish her, she'd dumped the cheating jerk, cashed in the honeymoon tickets to Hawaii she'd purchased, and escaped to southwestern Colorado for a fresh start.

Needing to get away and clear her head, she'd gifted herself an early birthday present and rented a yurt at the Stone River Guest Ranch in Aspen Ridge for a week.

Maybe she'd have the serenity she needed to decide if she should reopen her grandmother's artisan gift shop or sell the cottage that had been Callie's sanctuary since childhood.

Instead of donning the gorgeous wedding dress she should've been wearing that morning, she'd pulled on a pair of faded jeans, her favorite purple T-shirt, a pair of flip-flops, and faced the day with determination despite the state of her heart.

But that resolve took a nosedive when she ended up stranded on the side of an unfamiliar Colorado road with sketchy cell service.

She turned the key in the ignition once more, but this time, the dash lights didn't even come on.

"Now what?" Her words floated away in the light breeze that brushed across her face.

At least she was on Stone River property, if the map she'd downloaded to her phone was anything to go by.

Callie popped the hood on the ten-year-old blue VW Bug she'd inherited from her grandmother. Hand on her hip, she stared at the foreign-looking parts under the hood.

Why hadn't she paid attention when her dad had offered to give her a basic course in car maintenance?

She pulled her cell phone out of her back pocket once again and checked for any sign of service.

Still nothing.

Early June sunshine warmed the top of her head as she turned and leaned a hip against the car's fender. Folding her arms over her chest, she gazed at the snow-tipped mountains shouldering a sapphire sky and towering over fenced green pastures where pink, purple and yellow wildflowers swayed in the breeze. Cattle and horses in the distance lifted their heads, then returned to their grazing.

She could see for miles—or at least that was how it seemed—yet there wasn't a person in sight. Well, standing on the side of the road wouldn't solve her problems.

Callie slammed the hood shut, then opened the trunk. She retrieved her roller bag and her black art case. After slipping her favorite navy ball cap on her head and pulling her dark ponytail through the back, she pocketed her phone and keys. She grabbed her water bottle, locked the door and headed for the dirt road that would lead her to the tranquil retreat promised on the Stone River Ranch website.

Hopefully.

Ten minutes later, she rolled her shoulders, wiped the sweat from her forehead, then drained the rest of her water. Even though it wasn't even noon, the sun heated her skin. She shoved the empty bottle in the top of her bulging suitcase.

As she wheeled it again in front of her, one of the corners banged against a rock. The case lurched forward, then fell sideways. Callie stumbled but caught herself from face-planting in the dirt. A small black wheel lay on its side next to her purple bag.

"Perfect."

Heaving a sigh, Callie shoved the broken wheel in her pocket, then maneuvered the bag, pulling it behind her.

At the sound of an approaching vehicle, she moved to the edge of the road. Instead of driving past her, a black Ford Explorer pulled ahead and stopped.

Callie's fingers tightened on the handle.

The door opened, and a tall man climbed out and strode over to her, wearing aviator sunglasses and a backwards baseball hat covering short dark brown hair. His navy T-shirt emphasized his broad chest and muscled arms. Faded jeans clung to muscular thighs. And his dusty boots weren't for show.

She was definitely in cowboy country.

"Hey, there. You the owner of the blue Volkswagen back there?" Half turning, he jerked a thumb over his shoulder.

Pulling her suitcase in front of her, she nodded. "My car stalled out on my way to the Stone River Guest Ranch. I'm renting a yurt for the week."

"Well, then, it looks like I came along at the right time." He pulled off his sunglasses, revealing blue eyes, and hooked the arm over the collar of his T-shirt. He held out a calloused hand. "Wyatt Stone. My parents own this spread."

Wyatt Stone.

Her secret crush from her early high school years.

As a teenager, she'd held on to hope he'd see her as more than Ada Morgan's city-girl granddaughter who visited Aspen Ridge during the summer and holidays.

But he'd had eyes only for Linnea Douglas, whose parents owned the animal shelter next to Gram's cottage.

"Hey, Wyatt." She reached for his hand, then jerked hers back and wiped her grimy fingers on the leg of her jeans. "Sorry, my hand's a bit grubby from messing under the hood." Then she pulled off her own sunglasses. "It's me, Callie. Ada's granddaughter."

"Callie Morgan. Good to see you again." He smiled wide, deepening tiny lines bracketing his mouth, and nodded. His eyes softened. "I'm sorry I couldn't do more than express my condolences at your grandma's funeral."

"No worries. There was a line out the door." She dropped her gaze to her feet, then looked up at him again. "Good to see you too. How are you doing?"

"A little better than you, it seems. Know much about cars?" He shot her another grin.

She tightened her hands on the handle of her suitcase once again. "I can pump my own gas and check the tire pressure. That's about it."

"Let me give you a lift, and I'll see what I can do." He reached for her suitcase.

"I really appreciate it. I promise—you won't hear a peep from me for the rest of my stay."

"No need for that. We want everyone to feel welcomed. Once the rest of our guests arrive tomorrow, we'll have plenty of activities for you to enjoy."

"What I need most is solitude. I have some tough decisions to make. Gram left me the cottage that housed her gift shop. I have to decide if I'm going to keep it or sell it."

"Ada was quite a lady. Her death left a big hole in the community She'd been friends with my family for a long time. My mom loved her stained glass classes." Wyatt opened the lift gate and set her suitcase in the back.

She handed him the art case. "She mentioned you guys a lot."

He closed the lift gate, then rounded the passenger side of his SUV and opened the door. "Hop in, and we'll see what's going on with your car."

Callie eyed the black SUV. "Isn't there an unwritten rule or something that cowboys are required to drive pickup trucks?"

"Nah, those are just guidelines." He flashed her another lopsided grin. "Actually, the SUV belonged to my wife, and it's easier for my daughter to climb in and out of. I use the ranch truck when necessary." He nodded to the small child buckled in a car seat in the middle of the back seat. "Callie, this is my daughter, Mia. Mia, say hi to Callie. She's Miss Ada's granddaughter."

"Hi." The little girl lifted a small hand, then buried her face in the pink elephant clutched in her arms.

"Hi, Mia." Callie slid onto the seat, then faced Wyatt's daughter. The little girl wore pink plastic sunglasses, and her blond hair had been pulled back into two ponytails. "I like your elephant. What's her name?"

"Ella. Today's my birthday. I'm three." She held up three pudgy fingers.

"Ella the Elephant. I love that. And happy birthday. Three is a fun age."

"You know about being three?"

Callie smiled. "A long time ago."

Wyatt slid behind the wheel and closed the door. "Three going on thirteen. Sweet as frosting and stubborn as a bull."

Callie laughed. "You and your wife must have your hands full."

"We… I mean, I'm…my wife passed away." The rich timbre of his voice lowered to nearly a whisper as his neck reddened.

The look on his face had her wishing she could snatch back her words.

"Come to think of it, Gram did mention your loss. With everything happening the last few months, it slipped my mind. I'm so sorry." She dropped her gaze to her hands and rubbed dirt off her index finger as heat warmed her cheeks.

"Thanks." He started the engine and pulled onto the road. As they drove back to the car, her rescuer remained quiet after she'd mentioned his late wife.

The familiar-looking Bug came into view. She'd barely gotten it on the side of the road before it shut down.

Wyatt glanced at her. "Wait—is that your grandma's car?"

"I inherited the car along with her cottage. Didn't make sense to keep two cars, so I sold mine. Maybe I got rid of the wrong one."

"I thought the Bug looked familiar. If so, then no need for me to look under the hood. The alternator needs to be replaced. Ada wouldn't let me fix it for her. Stubborn. Then she got sick... So, what happened before it broke down?"

Callie lifted a shoulder. "I'd just headed through the gate when the dashboard lights came on, blinked off, then the car quit. I barely had enough power to get it to the side of the road."

"Yep, sounds like the alternator." Wyatt pulled alongside the pasture fence, parked, and reached for his door handle. "Let's see if I'm right." Then he turned to Mia. "Stay put, Peanut. I'll be right back."

"Okay, Daddy."

Callie climbed out of the SUV and followed Wyatt to her car.

He lifted the hood, jiggled something, then peered at her. "Try and start it."

Callie slid behind the wheel and turned the key. The engine caught for a second then died. She tried again, but this time, the engine didn't even turn over.

Wyatt closed the hood and wiped his hands on his jeans. Then he rested an arm on Callie's open, driver's-side door. "Just as I figured, the alternator's shot. I'll load up the rest of your stuff and give you a lift to your yurt. Then I'll give Gavin Copeland a call and get it towed to his garage in town."

"I don't want to be a bother. I can take care of it."

"It's no bother at all."

She slid her sunglasses back in place. "Good thing I don't have plans to do much more than work at the cottage or start a new painting this week. Or maybe take that trail ride."

"Right—you're an artist like your grandma. I'd forgotten that."

She unlocked the trunk, and he reached for another small suitcase the same time she did. His fingers covered hers, then he jerked his hand back. "Sorry." He shot her a grin. "So, you like to ride?"

"Like to?" She shrugged, then laughed. "I've spent most of my life living near cities. I've ridden a time or two with some assistance, but I'm certainly no pro. When I came to Aspen Ridge to care for Gram after her stroke, I didn't have much time to leave town, let alone get on a horse. Now that I've moved here, I need to find a job as soon as possible so any horse riding will be limited to what the guest ranch offers this upcoming week."

"You moved to Aspen Ridge?" He set her suitcase next to the other one in the back of his SUV, then leaned against the rear quarter panel, crossed his ankles, and folded his arms over his chest. "What kind of job are you looking for?"

She diverted her eyes from the way the T-shirt material stretched over his shoulders. "Anything that pays a decent wage. I have degrees in art history and elementary education, but I'm not looking to head back to the classroom anytime soon."

"Have any management experience?"

She squinted against the sun reflecting off the back window and shielded her eyes. "Spent my college summers being a counselor and organizing activities for a kids' camp. Does that count?"

"It does to me. Interested in a job?"

Her eyes widened. "Seriously?"

"My oldest sister planned to oversee our family's guest ranch, but she just had a baby. So I took over for her as director, but I have a lot on my plate as well. I'll supervise everything, but

I'd like to have a manager to help with the day-to-day. That way, Macey can devote her time to her family. The job's yours if you want it. Unless you're looking for something closer to the city."

"I moved to Aspen Ridge for a fresh start. I need open spaces and plenty of sunshine." She cocked her head. "But why would you offer a job to someone you picked up on the side of the road? I could be a serial killer for all you know."

He laughed, a deep sound that rumbled low in his chest. "Picked up? You're not some kind of empty bottle someone tossed out the window."

After her ex's infidelity, she felt tossed aside.

"We used to hang out when we were younger, and the Callie I once knew wasn't much of a serial killer."

"I'm not much of anything these days. Gram's death has been…tough." Her throat thickened as her vision blurred. Again. Grateful for her sunglasses shielding her eyes, she rolled them upward to prevent unexpected tears from spilling out her pain. "Thanks for the offer. I'll take it."

"Listen. I know what it's like to lose someone you love." Wyatt's voice lowered and held compassion that threatened to break the hold on her emotions. He held out his large hand. "Give me your phone, and I'll add my number. You can relax tonight, then we can work out the details in the next day or so."

"Sounds good." She pulled her phone and handed it to him. "Thanks for stopping. I couldn't get a cell signal and wasn't sure what to do."

"Depending on your provider, service can be spotty on the ranch. We do have Wi-Fi for guests, so you can connect to that. I have your information packet and keys at the lodge. I'll grab those, then you can get settled."

Settled.

She hadn't felt that in months. Not since the call after Christmas about Gram's stroke that landed her in the hospital, and then learning her fiancé had cheated on her while she'd taken a short leave to care for Gram.

She'd resigned from her teaching position, closed up her apartment, and left the city to start over in a newish town.

And she'd never felt more alone.

Hopefully, this was just what she needed to make the right decision about Gram's shop. She promised to reopen, but in order to do so, the place needed some renovations. And that took money she didn't have.

As her parents continually reminded her—*God will provide.*

Perhaps working for the Stone family for the summer was just what her heart needed. Then she could focus on where to go from there.

Had God answered her prayers by allowing her car to break down?

Only one way to find out.

The anniversary of his wife's death always hit Wyatt Stone in the gut. Three years later, it was no exception.

Maybe that was why he'd stumbled over his marital status when Callie mentioned his wife. Why was it still an issue?

Because he didn't want to believe it was true. To be reminded of what he'd lost. He and Mia. But instead of dwelling on that, he needed to focus on what he'd gained.

His eyes shifted to the rearview mirror where his daughter sat in her car seat with Ella tucked in her tiny arms and her eyes watching Callie.

With today also being Mia's birthday, she deserved to be celebrated even if he wanted nothing more than to forget about the date on the calendar. With everything going on, he didn't have time to dwell on his pain.

Midmorning sunshine glinted off the silvery, snow-capped peaks of the San Juan Mountains towering over the valley of his family's cattle ranch as he passed the horseshoe drive lined with tall, green-leafed aspens in front of his parents' stone-and-timber ranch house.

At the fork, he took the left road and pulled

into the small gravel lot next to the log-sided lodge with an evergreen metal roof.

Adirondack chairs sat on a stained wrap-around deck and faced the water. A short trail took guests to the four yurts—cylindrical, tent-like structures on platforms—nestled in their private groves of aspens and pines.

After cutting the engine, he unbuckled Mia from her car seat. She scrambled down and raced for the front door, her blond ponytails bouncing against her shoulders.

"Nana! Papa! I'm here. Can we have my party now?"

Laughing softly, Wyatt rounded the front to open Callie's door, but she beat him to it.

He jerked his head toward the lodge. "Come in and say hi to my folks. I'll grab your paperwork then show you to your yurt."

"Thanks, but I don't mind waiting out here. I don't want to intrude."

Following Mia, he grabbed the front door before it slammed shut and held it open. "You won't be, and they'll want to see you."

They stepped into the expansive room with a gleaming floor. Sunshine spilled through arched windows and highlighted the polished wood planks with darkened knots lining the walls. Three deep brown overstuffed leather couches formed a boxy U in front of a floor-to-ceiling stone fireplace.

To the left, half a dozen round tables with chairs dotted the dining area. A large kitchen showed stainless appliances and a deep farmhouse-style sink. A timber-planked staircase opened into a loft that overlooked the first floor.

Soft music and quiet laughter came from the open kitchen where his parents stood at the sink on either side of Mia, who had pulled up a stool to help.

Callie removed her sunglasses, glanced at the exposed beam ceiling, then looked at him. "This is gorgeous."

"Thanks. My brother-in-law's crew finished it last month. The wood used on the walls and floor was planed from downed trees on Stone River property." He nodded toward the kitchen. "Let's say hi."

A light breeze blew through the open window above the sink and stirred the blue-and-white striped curtains.

His dad stood with his back to them as he helped Mia wash red and yellow bell peppers under the running water.

"Hey, Dad. What's going on?" Wyatt moved behind Mia.

Dad glanced at him. "Hey, Wy. Prepping for tomorrow night's welcome dinner. With Mia's party this afternoon, church tomorrow morning, and then preparing for everyone's arrival, there won't be much time later."

"Hey, Mom." Wyatt dropped a kiss on his mother's cheek, then turned to Callie. "You guys remember Callie Morgan?"

"Hi, honey." Mom wiped her hands on the blue dish towel hanging from the oven door and moved around him. She pulled Callie into a hug. "It's good to see you again, Callie."

"You too, Mrs. Stone."

"Please call me Nora. You remember my husband, Deacon?" She handed the towel to Dad, and he dried his hands.

"Of course. Good morning."

"Morning, Callie." His father extended a hand, and she took it. "Heard you rented one of the yurts. How about a cup of coffee?"

Callie glanced at Wyatt.

Holding the stool as Mia climbed down, he lifted a shoulder. "Unless you're in a hurry to get unpacked, you're welcome to hang out for a few minutes."

She nodded to his dad. "Okay, then. Sure, thanks."

Wyatt pulled two coffee cups out of the oak cabinet and filled them from the full pot next to the stove. Inhaling the scent of the dark roast, he handed one to Callie.

"Thanks." Smiling, she took it and added creamer that Dad slid closer to her.

"Callie, how about if Mia and I give you a tour of the lodge?" Mom reached for Mia's hand.

"Mind if I bring my coffee?" Callie lifted her cup.

"Not at all."

Once they were out of earshot, Wyatt palmed his mug and moved next to his dad. "I had a talk with my in-laws this morning when I picked up Mia."

"Yeah? What's going on? Everything okay with Ray and Irene?" Dad unrolled the sleeves on his red plaid Western shirt, then snapped the cuffs closed. "Let's head outside and get the wood split for tomorrow night's campfire."

Wyatt dropped his gaze to his mug, swirled the black coffee to break up his reflection, then drained his cup. He set it on the counter, then followed his dad out the back door. "I heard a rumor their horse rescue was in danger of being shut down due to lack of funds. I offered to partner with them to keep it going."

"I hadn't heard that about the horse rescue." Rounding the back of the lodge, his dad pulled keys from his front pocket and unlocked a small work shed. He threw both doors open, turned on the lights, and nodded to the black-and-yellow machine against the wall. "Give me a hand, will you?"

They wheeled the portable wood splitter outside next to a pile of cut-up logs. Dad pulled the cord, and the machine rumbled to life.

Wyatt grabbed two pairs of work gloves off one of the shelves and tossed a pair to his dad, who caught them in one hand. He set a log on the tray.

Dad moved the lever forward as the blade divided the wood in two. "You've mentioned wanting to take it over should it become too much for Ray to do on his own."

"I asked them about it. Ray was his usual crusty self and said I had no business listening to rumors. But Irene confirmed it was true. Ray resists the idea of monthly sponsors. Their donors haven't been as giving as in the past." Wyatt stacked the split wood on a low pile by the shed and added another log to the tray. "She said if something doesn't change soon, they may have to sell. Today's hard enough with the anniversary of Linnea's death. I don't want them stressing about this too."

"Their ranch has been in the Douglas family for as long as Stone River's been a part of ours." Dad added another log to the tray and split it. "What can we do to help?"

That was so like Dad—quick to step in and lend a hand.

"Talk to Ray. He listens to you. Show him how a partnership with Stone River—if you'd be willing—could benefit all of us. Linnea always wanted to turn the rescue into a horse sanctuary. With Mia being their only granddaughter, I don't want her to lose her mother's legacy."

"We don't want that either." Dad cut the power and leveled Wyatt with a compassionate look. "You doing okay today? We loved Linnea too, you know."

Despite the sudden thickening in his throat and pressure behind his eyes, Wyatt blinked several times and nodded. "I have to be. No time for anything else."

"No one would blame you if you weren't."

"Thanks. I'm good." Wyatt stacked the remaining wood on the pile.

"You sure taking on the horse rescue won't be too much? You just took over the guest ranch. Between that, helping Bear and me with chores, leading the single fathers support group and caring for Mia, you don't want to spread yourself too thin."

Yeah, that had crossed his mind too, but he didn't dare voice it. He didn't need his parents or anyone else worrying about him needlessly.

"I'll handle it. I won't let any of you down. I promise."

Dad dropped a hand on Wyatt's shoulder and

squeezed. "You're not alone, son. We're all here to help. Ray's always been like a brother to me. I'll talk to him and see what he thinks about a partnership with us."

"Thanks, Dad. I appreciate it. I don't want to add more work for you or Bear, especially since he's trying to get his rehabilitation ranch up and running. If we do partner with the rescue, then we could consider using the horses for the riding program we've been wanting to start. I can use some of Linnea's life insurance money to buy into the rescue."

Dad pulled off his gloves and slapped them against his thigh. "You know Ray won't go for that. It's earmarked for Mia's future."

"And turning the rescue into a sanctuary would be part of that future. I know it's what Linnea would want."

Dad lifted the end of the splitter and pulled it back into the shed. "If we use the horses for the riding program, they'll need to be retrained first. Many of them have been abandoned or abused and have serious trust issues."

Wyatt removed his gloves, then wiped his sweaty face with the hem of his T-shirt. He followed his dad inside the shed and grabbed a rake off the wall. "Yes, but they'll also be protected from future kill lots and have a renewed purpose again."

Something he'd desperately been searching for himself since losing the love of his life.

"Troy Branson, one of the guys in my single fathers' group, is a horse trainer looking to expand his business. We could send some work his way." Wyatt headed outside and raked a small pile of shavings toward the woodpile.

"Pray about it, son. See where God's leading you. Taking on the rescue is a big responsibility, but we'll back you up. You know that. Let's head back inside the lodge. I need to finish cutting the peppers for tomorrow night's welcome dinner."

Yes, he knew he had his family behind him. Having their support was the only way he could've left the Marine Corps after losing his wife tragically during childbirth. The way they'd stepped in to help care for Mia when he could barely care for himself had put him in their debt.

One he hoped to repay someday.

"Thanks, Dad. I appreciate it." Wyatt followed him back up the deck and into the lodge kitchen.

The front door opened, sending a stream of sunshine across the floor along with female laughter.

Mom, Callie and Mia stepped inside followed by his older sister, Macey, who slid her sunglasses to the top of her head as she snuggled her newborn son against her chest. Wrapped in a receiving blanket covered in horseshoes, the baby was barely visible. Wyatt could see only his nephew's dark hair.

Wyatt washed his hands, then left the kitchen and crossed the room. He reached for the newborn. "Come see your favorite uncle, little guy." He glanced at his sister as he cradled the baby against his chest. "My first day on the job and you're already checking up on me?"

Macey laughed and gave him a playful shove. "Hardly. I'm heading into town to meet up with Cole. He took Lexi to the doctor for a checkup. Then we're meeting Piper and Everly for lunch. I wanted to double-check with Mom to see if things had changed and she could join us." She glanced at Callie. "Cole's my husband, Piper is Bear's wife, and Everly is our baby sister."

Callie nodded.

Their mother chimed in. "Wish I could, honey, but I promised your Aunt Lynetta I'd help at the diner this afternoon. One of her servers quit last week, and she hasn't found someone to replace her yet."

Callie moved next to him, smelling of fresh air and sunshine. She pulled back the blanket and caressed the baby's cheek. "He's precious. What's his name?"

His sister's eyes softened. "Thanks. We adore him. Deacon Cole, or DC as his papa started calling him." She shot a look at Dad. "He's only a couple of weeks old."

Callie glanced at Wyatt. "Mind if I hold him?"

"Not at all." He released his nephew into her arms.

She embraced the baby and swayed gently from side to side.

Macey nudged Wyatt's shoulder. "Callie said you hired her to manage the guest ranch."

He glanced at Callie, who shifted Baby Deacon to her shoulder and rubbed his back. "She needed a job, and I needed an assistant, so it seemed like a good idea. Plus, it saves me the hassle of finding people to interview."

Wyatt looked at Callie. "Sorry. I meant for this to be a quick stop."

She grinned. "Don't worry about me. Holding this baby is the most fun I've had in a while."

Wyatt cleared his throat. "If you'd like, I can give you a tour and talk about our expectations for the guest ranch."

"The tour sounds good too, but I don't want to keep you from your family, especially since today is Mia's birthday." She rubbed her cheek over the baby's head.

"You took a lot off my plate by agreeing to be the manager for the summer. By the way, Mia will be going with us as well."

"Sounds good. She's adorable." She returned

the baby back to Macey, then jerked her head toward the front door. "If you direct me to where I'll be staying, I'll change into something more suitable for walking."

Callie looked so natural with his nephew in her arms. She'd make a great mom someday.

Wyatt's chest tightened as he ran his thumb over the back of his platinum wedding band. He and Linnea had wanted a handful of kids, but her sudden death had wrecked that dream.

He wouldn't find another woman like her, so why bother looking?

He couldn't change things, no matter how much he wanted to. So he'd power through the day as he'd been doing every day for the past three years.

Besides, when would he have time for romance with his busy schedule? Someday, maybe, he'd change his mind about falling in love again. But that was doubtful. He couldn't risk losing someone else he loved. He didn't know if he could recover a second time.

For now, he'd focus on making the summer season at the guest ranch a success. He hoped hiring Callie was the first of many good decisions. Only time would tell, but he had a feeling this was going to be a memorable summer. For all of them.

Chapter Two

~

If he wanted his dad to seriously consider partnering with the Douglas ranch, then Wyatt needed to prove himself more than ever and show his family he was capable of managing his responsibilities.

All of them.

The last thing he wanted was to cost his daughter her legacy.

But he couldn't dwell on that right now. He needed to give Callie a tour to confirm he'd made the right choice in hiring her.

His job offer had been off the cuff, and her acceptance had surprised him. At least he'd have much-needed help to ensure their first summer at the guest ranch was a success.

No way was he about to let that venture fall apart, especially after the time and money his family had invested in getting it up and running.

He traded his SUV for the utility vehicle his parents had driven to the guest ranch, which would be easier for taking Callie on the tour.

Outside her yurt, he braked and hopped out. He released Mia's seat belt and helped her down.

The sun caught him in the eye, and he patted the collar of his T-shirt for his sunglasses. He slipped them on his face and adjusted the brim of his cowboy hat.

Mia tugged on his hand. "Can we go see Uncle Bear?"

"We'll drive by his place, sweetheart, but we won't be able to stop. Uncle Bear, Aunt Piper and Avery went away for the day."

Still clutching her pink elephant in the crook of her elbow, Mia cocked her head, tapped her chin, then nodded. "Will they be at my party?"

"Yes, they'll be there tonight."

"Yay!"

The door to the yurt opened, and Callie stepped out wearing the same purple T-shirt and faded jeans that hugged her curves, but she'd exchanged her flip-flops for gray sneakers. Her navy ball cap covered her dark hair, giving him only a glimpse of the ponytail brushing her shoulders. She wore the same dark sunglasses she'd had on earlier. At the lodge, he'd seen her eyes were the same dark brown as he remembered.

He lifted a hand, then reached for Mia's. They headed toward her. "Hello, again."

"Hey." Her eyes shifted from him to Mia. "Hi, Mia."

"Hi." Her little voice chirped, then she buried her face in Wyatt's leg.

Wyatt nodded toward the Gator. "I figured we'd drive around different parts of the ranch so you could get a feel of what's here."

"Sounds good to me." Callie rounded the front and climbed in the passenger seat.

Mia climbed in behind the driver's seat, and Wyatt helped her with the seat belt buckle. Then he slid behind the wheel and did a U-turn in the middle of the dirt road. He glanced at Callie. "What do you know about our ranch?"

She grabbed the frame as they bounced over a rut in the road. "Just what I've read online and learned from my grandma."

"I'll give you a refresher. Feel free to ask questions." At her nod, he continued. "My great-grandparents started the ranch, then it was handed down to my dad's parents. They were killed by a drunk driver just over ten years ago, so Dad took over the ranch with all of us helping out. Macey and Cole got married not quite a year ago and were a bit surprised to learn they were going to have a baby so soon. Cole also has an adorable daughter from his first marriage. Bear and Piper got married a few months ago, and Bear is raising Piper's daughter, Avery, as his own."

"Your family's grown so quickly over the last

year or so. I met Cole and Piper at Gram's funeral." Callie's fingers tightened on the frame as they hit through another rut in the road.

"Daddy, this road is bouncy." Mia's laughter from the back seat warmed his heart.

He turned and grinned. "Hold on tight, Peanut. But don't worry—Daddy will keep you safe."

He looked at Callie. "Sorry about that. The recent spring rains made a mess of the roads, and we haven't had time to fill in the holes."

"No worries. I saw Everly at Gram's funeral as well, but you have another sister, right?"

"Yes, Mallory. She's in the navy, currently stationed in Virginia. She has a six-year-old son, Tanner. She's scheduled to be discharged at the end of the summer. Everly teaches second grade at Aspen Ridge Elementary and helps Mom with cleaning the yurts and preparing meals for our guests."

"Your family has a lot going on."

"One of the reasons I took over the guest ranch. Dad had a terrible bout of pneumonia little over a year ago, and I'm not so sure he ever fully recovered. I don't want him or my mom overdoing it."

"It's great the way you watch over each other."

"That's what our family does. They were there for me when my wife died, and I had an infant with no clue how to care for her." Wyatt lifted a shoulder. "Your family seems pretty close too."

"We are, but being so far apart these days, we stay connected by video chatting every week. My younger brothers, who are fraternal twins, will start med school in Denver in the fall."

"Wesley and Trevor, right?"

"Good memory. I don't know if you remember or not, but my parents are missionaries in South America." Callie clasped her hands and blew out a breath. "I'm the one who's a bit at loose ends these days. The life I'd planned isn't living up to my expectations."

He wanted to ask more about the life she'd planned, but he didn't want to pry.

But he got it—his life hadn't gone the way he'd expected either.

Wyatt swung down the road leading to his brother's cabin. "This road isn't marked, and we discourage our guests from walking this way. It's Bear's property, and we need to respect his and Piper's privacy."

The trees gave away to a clearing that showcased a wood-sided cabin topped with a dark green metal roof and matching shutters.

"Wow, that's gorgeous."

"Yeah, it's a pretty sweet place. Bear built it from his rodeo earnings, but now he's retired from bull riding. He and Piper are transforming their property into a small rehab ranch for cowboys with traumatic brain injuries in memory of Piper's late husband, who was also Bear's best friend."

"What an incredible thing to do."

"They're pretty incredible people." Wyatt turned the Gator around and headed back toward the ranch. "If you're not bored yet, Mia and I will take you to Stone River, my family's working ranch."

"Bored? Not likely. This place is perfect." Callie turned in her seat. "Thanks for allowing me to come along, Mia."

Wyatt smiled at the way Callie tried to include his daughter.

"Want to meet the horses?"

Callie's eyes widened as she clasped her hands together. Her knuckles whitened. "Horses?"

"Yes, those large animals we ride in these parts."

She shot him a mock glare. "I know what a horse is…"

"They make you nervous?"

She didn't respond for a moment, then glanced at him. "They're just so big."

They passed the ranch house, the hoop barn, and stopped between the arena and the horse barn.

"Big, yes. But also gentle." Wyatt climbed out

from behind the wheel, then released Mia's seat belt. "Okay, gang. Everybody out."

Callie stepped out but kept her hand tightened around the frame of the Gator.

Wyatt motioned toward the barn. "Let's head inside, and I'll introduce you. We don't have a barn built near the guest ranch yet. For now, we tack them up here and transport them to the guest ranch when we have rides scheduled."

Her steps slowed, but he'd wait. She wasn't the first guest to be nervous around the animals.

They stepped inside the barn, and Wyatt flipped on the light.

"How many horses do you have?" Callie stood next to the tack room, her arms hugging her stomach.

Scents of hay mingled with warm animals. Flies buzzed as the horses nickered upon their arrival.

"Eight, but we have room for ten in this barn. We're hoping to expand, but that depends on how the summer goes."

"Why's that?" Then she scrunched her face. "Sorry. None of my business."

He laughed. "You're fine. I'm trying to convince my father-in-law to allow me to partner with his horse rescue. I'd love to turn it into a sanctuary, then retrain the horses for a riding program we'd like to set up here at Stone River."

Callie took another step into the barn. "You Stones trying to corner the market on admirable endeavors?"

He grinned again. "Just obeying God's call for our ranch and resources." He reached into a bucket for a handful of treats, then knelt in front of Mia and put a few in the palm of her hand. "Show Callie how well Patience takes her treats."

She hurried over to his mother's mare's stall and called for the chestnut-colored horse. Patience lowered her muzzle and nudged the top of Mia's head.

Mia giggled and patted the horse's nose, then held a treat in her hand. Patience took it, causing Mia to laugh again as she wiped her hands on her denim shorts. "That tickles, Daddy."

As they passed each horse, Wyatt named them and gave them a treat. They greeted him by nudging him with their muzzles. He rubbed their foreheads as they swished flies away with their tails.

"I thought horses spent most of their time outside."

"Generally, yes. Depends on the weather too. This week is calling for some pretty high temps, especially for this early in the summer, so we bring them in each morning and feed them. They hang out in the barn during the day to avoid the flies and the heat. Then we feed them and let them out for the night when it's cooler and the flies aren't biting. While they're in the pasture, we clean their stalls and put down fresh bedding."

He handed her a small apple then held his palm flat. "Hold your hand like this and let Ranger take it from you."

Callie's eyes widened. Did she take a step back? She hadn't said much once they entered the barn. Her tense shoulders and tight jaw showed she wasn't as relaxed around horses as she maybe wanted him to think. She kept a cautious distance from the stalls, particularly when the horses extended their heads over the top of the stall doors. "You sure it's okay?"

"Ranger's a big boy, but he has a gentle heart. He's been my horse since I was in high school. He won't bite you, I promise."

Her fingers curled around the apple as she remained rooted where she stood in the middle of the aisle. She eyed Ranger, then glanced at Wyatt. "You guys stay pretty busy, don't you?"

He pressed a shoulder against Ranger's stall door. "There's always something that needs to be done on the ranch."

"You have cattle, too? I think I read that on your website."

"We have about a hundred head. We had more,

but sold some off to keep the ranch afloat a year or so ago when we hit a rough patch. The livestock barn is on the other side of this one. Mom has chickens too. Plus, we acquired a few sheep and a couple of small goats this past spring." Wyatt rubbed Ranger's forehead once more and gestured for Callie to come closer. "He won't bite you. I promise."

"Ranger is nice, Callie. He won't hurt you." Mia tugged on Callie's hand and tried to pull her closer to the horse.

Callie glanced at his daughter, smiled tightly, then blew out a breath and took a step forward. She held out her hand as Wyatt directed, and Ranger took the fruit gently.

"Good boy." Wyatt patted the side of the black stallion's neck.

"That wasn't so bad."

Was she talking to him...or herself?

Callie took a step back, wiped her hand on her jeans and turned to him, an overly bright smile in place. "So, what will my responsibilities be?"

He bit back a smile, pulled a folded sheet of paper out of his back pocket and handed it to Callie. "As I mentioned, tomorrow is our first official opening for the summer season. This past spring, we had a family or two as well as some outdoor enthusiasts who traveled to the area to fish and hunt. This is the overview that we created."

She read it over, then looked at him. "So you'll want me available from eight in the morning until six in the evening?"

Wyatt reached for Ranger's water bucket and refilled it. "We want to be present for part of the day, but you'll have time for yourself. When new guests arrive each week, we'll greet them and provide them with registration packets that outline our policies and procedures and a list of activities for the week. Tomorrow night, we'll have a campfire, introduce everyone, and answer any questions. I'd love for you to be available for that."

"Yes, of course. How do you do the meals?"

"Family-style breakfast is offered each morning at eight in the lodge, with lunch at noon, and dinner at six. Guests can participate or do their own cooking in their yurts. You're welcome to eat with the guests, the staff, or even my family. We'll end each day with a campfire and s'mores. Throughout the day, we offer organized activities such as trail riding, kayaking and other water sports, archery and fishing. Dad will give tours of the ranch, including a petting zoo for the kids. Macey will be offering photography walks. Bear and I will oversee the trail riding and water sports. Everly planned some family-friendly activities that we've included, such as geocaching, hiking and craft projects. My parents handle the finances."

"You all pitch in."

"We do, but we still need someone to manage the day-to-day details and ensure people are where they're supposed to be. Does this sound like something you're still interested in doing?"

"Yes, I think so as long as you don't mind me being in town during my free time. I want to do as much as I can in Gram's shop."

"Not at all. Your time is your own." Wyatt motioned for them to follow him outside. "You're not planning to return to teaching in the fall?"

"Not if I can help it." She lowered her eyes, but not before he caught the shadow that passed over them. "I love children, and my time as a teacher taught me a lot, but it's not my passion."

"What is?"

"My art. Being creative in a self-expressive way, not teaching to a curriculum. I'd love to teach the kinds of art classes Gram and I always talked about doing together—pottery, stained glass, watercolors. That kind of thing."

Outside, he slid his sunglasses back on his face. "If you love art so much, how'd you end up in the classroom?"

"My parents wanted me to have a reliable job

to support myself. They didn't want me to be a starving artist."

"I can appreciate that." He ran a hand over the back of his neck. "You're seriously overqualified for this position. Are you sure it's something you want to do?"

"It's exactly what I need right now. No long-term commitments. Plus, it's a step outside my comfort zone. Hopefully, by the end of summer, I'll have the gift shop open and can move onto the next phase of keeping my promise to my grandmother."

"Okay, then. Welcome to the ranch." Wyatt stuck out his hand, and she shook it, her skin soft against his calloused fingers.

Mia pressed her head against Wyatt's leg. "Daddy, I'm tired."

He lifted her in his arms and pressed a kiss against her forehead. "Okay, Peanut. Let's get you down for a nap." He looked at Callie. "Mind if we head back? That way, you can relax and have a peaceful afternoon."

She shook her head. "Not at all. I've enjoyed the tour. Thank you."

They climbed back into the utility vehicle and headed back to the guest ranch.

As Wyatt stopped in front of Callie's yurt, his phone vibrated in his front pocket. He dug it out, and his mother-in-law's number appeared on the screen.

"Who is it, Daddy?"

"It's Grammy, sweetie." He showed her the screen, then tapped the accept button. "Mama D, what's up?"

"Wyatt, I'm in the ER with Ray. He took a nasty fall and hurt his leg." Her words came out in a rush.

Eyeing Mia, who stared at him, Wyatt forced a calm tone. His fingers tightened around the phone. "How bad is it?"

"They're talking surgery. We're still in the emergency department at Aspen Ridge General, but they're talking about life-flighting him to Durango. I hate to ask, especially today, but could you pick me up so I can get my car? I rode over in the ambulance." The catch in her voice tugged at Wyatt's chest.

"Mom and Dad aren't home. Let me see who's available to care for Mia, then I'll be in."

"Thank you so much, Wyatt. You have no idea how much this means to me."

"Anything for you, Mama D. You know that." He ended the call and gripped the phone. Then he turned to Callie. "Sorry to cut this short, but I need to head into town."

"Everything okay?"

Wyatt's jaw tightened as he turned. Certain

Mia couldn't see him, he gave a brief shake of his head. "I need to stop by the ranch and see if one of my sisters is around to watch Mia. My in-laws need me at the hospital."

"I'm sorry." Callie's eyes softened as they drifted toward his daughter. "I can do it."

"You can do what?"

"I can care for Mia until you get back."

"Thanks, I appreciate it. Problem is, I don't know when that will be."

She lifted a shoulder. "No worries. I don't have plans anyway."

"But you're on vacation."

"A vacation that ends tomorrow afternoon, remember? Besides, it sounds like you need to leave right away."

"I do, but you just met Mia this morning. I don't want her to be too much or anything."

"Wyatt, listen. I understand your hesitation, but I do have state clearances. Plus, I've spent the last six years teaching art classes to elementary students. If I can handle a group of twenty kids at a time, then I'm sure one little girl will be just fine."

While he believed her words, his heart had a hard time catching up with his head. But he was wasting time wrestling with his indecision. "As long as you're sure. I'll give Mom a call and ask her to pick Mia up when she returns to the ranch. That way you're not tied down for the rest of the day."

Callie pressed a hand against his arm. "Relax, okay? I can handle this."

Wyatt stared at her narrow fingers with unpolished, trimmed nails. Her gentle touch warmed his skin. He blew out a breath and nodded. Then he knelt in front of his daughter and touched her face. "Hey, Peanut. I have to go into town and help Grammy with something. Would you like to stay with Callie until Nana can pick you up?"

"What about my birthday party? I wanna go see Grammy too."

"Sorry, sweetie. Not right now. You'll see her very soon. And we will have your party as soon as I get back. I promise."

Her lip drooped as she pressed her head against his chest. "Okay."

"You sure you don't mind?" He glanced at Callie over the top of Mia's head.

"Not at all. With the way you helped me out this morning, I'm more than happy to return the favor."

He hadn't left his daughter with anyone other than family since she was born. He didn't doubt Callie's character. And the brief times he'd spent with her had left him with positive impressions.

He struggled with what it meant to lean on someone outside the family.

But he had no choice right now. Time to take a leap and put his trust—and his daughter—in Callie's capable hands.

Callie might have overestimated her skills.

While it was true she didn't have much experience with three-year-olds, she'd been counting on her years as an elementary school art teacher to keep Mia occupied while Wyatt headed into town.

She hadn't expected the little girl to burst into tears as soon as her father walked out the door.

For the past fifteen minutes, she'd rocked her and sung silly songs until the tears subsided, hoping the tired child would fall asleep.

Callie adjusted Mia in her arms and tried to find a more comfortable position on the coffee-colored microfiber couch that faced the window overlooking the lake.

Mia's chest rose and fell with each shallow shudder she breathed.

Maybe she should've suggested they hang out at Wyatt's place, so Mia would've been in a familiar setting. But she didn't want to intrude on his personal space since she was about to become his employee. And he'd seemed to be in a big hurry to leave.

She'd gotten the sense Wyatt wasn't too thrilled

about leaving his daughter in her care, but it sounded like he didn't have many options.

Now she needed something to interest Mia until her dad returned.

Callie spied her open art case on the island in the small kitchen area. What could she pull out to make the little girl smile? She brushed Mia's damp hair away from her face. "Mia, do you like to paint?"

Chin tucked down, the child nodded, her cheek scraping against Callie's T-shirt.

"Would you like to paint a picture for your daddy?"

Again, Mia nodded but remained quiet.

"Let's sit at the counter, and I'll get you some paint, okay?"

Another nod, but this time Mia stood and headed for the high-backed chairs pushed against the kitchen island.

Callie helped her onto the seat, then pulled out tubes of acrylic paint in blue, yellow and red, and squirted a quarter-size drop of each color on a paper plate.

Then she grabbed the nearly empty roll of paper towels, removed the remaining sheets and cut the roll into three-inch chunks. She folded two of the pieces into a triangle and a square, then left the other one circular. She found a small pad of mixed media paper and removed a sheet.

She sat next to Mia and put the paint in front of her. "You can dip these pieces into the paint and make shapes on your paper. How's that?"

Giving her a shy smile, Mia grabbed the square and plopped it in the middle of the red paint, then she pounced it on the paper. Then she reached for the circle and added blue paint to her paper.

Callie grabbed her hobby knife and trimmed a sheet of heavyweight, cold-pressed watercolor paper off the pad and set it on the island in front of her own chair.

She lightly sketched a little of what she'd seen on their tour—the mountains, the ranch house and a horse standing by the river. She retrieved her roll of brushes and tin of watercolors from her bag. Grabbing a spray bottle, she flipped open the lid to her paints and misted the pigments to hydrate them.

She glanced at Mia. "How you doing, kiddo?"

Mia held up her paper covered with splotchy shapes and splatters. "I made purple. It matches your shirt."

"You're right." Callie slid off the stool and moved to the sink. She filled her paint cup with water, then returned to her seat. She loaded her brush with water and applied it to the paper until it shone. "Can you tell me what colors make purple?"

Mia scrunched her face and looked at her paper. Then she shook her head.

Callie tapped the area where a red circle and a blue square overlapped. "Your red and blue mixed together to make purple."

"Yay. I want to do it again." Mia reached for another cardboard shape and mashed it into the muddied colors. "May I have more paint, please?"

"Nice manners. Of course you can." Callie reached for her acrylic paints and squeezed three more blobs on the plate.

Within minutes, Mia had her paper covered in colorful shapes. Not to mention her fingers and a couple of spots on her yellow T-shirt. Hopefully, the paint washed out.

Someone knocked on the screen door of the yurt, startling Callie. She whirled around and found Nora Stone standing on the deck. She wore a yellow Netta's Diner T-shirt with dark wash jeans. Her silvery-blond hair had been pulled up into a messy bun.

"Nana!" Mia scrambled off the chair, nearly falling to her knees. She rushed to the door then came to a stop. "Where's Daddy? Is it party time?"

Nora opened the door and peeked her head inside. "Mind if I come in?"

Callie waved her inside. "Not at all."

Opening the door wider, Nora stepped inside. Mia wrapped her arms around her grandmother's legs, and the woman lifted her into her arms and pressed a kiss against her cheek. "Hey, Birthday Girl." Then she turned her attention to Callie. "Thanks for helping out with Mia."

"I was glad to help. There were a few tears after Wyatt left, but I tried to distract her with some shape painting. She did very well." Callie lifted Mia's colorful paper off the counter and held it out to Nora. "It's still damp."

Nora smiled at Mia. "This is beautiful. Can I hang it on my fridge?"

Mia shook her head and pointed to Callie. "It's for her."

Callie pressed a hand against her chest. "Me? Thank you, Mia. I'll hang it on my fridge."

Nora handed the paper back to Callie. "Looks like you received your gift of teaching from your grandma. I loved her stained glass classes. She was a very kind and patient teacher. They were therapeutic as I grieved the loss of my in-laws. I'm happy to hear you're reopening her shop."

"It needs a lot of work. Gram always encouraged my love of art. I'm so sorry for your loss. I remember Gram talking about your in-laws."

"Thank you. And I'm sorry you're having to learn how to live without her. If you need to talk, give me a call or stop by the ranch house." Nora turned to Mia. "How about if we leave and let Callie get on with the rest of her day?"

Callie crouched in front of Mia and moved her hair away from her face. "Thanks for spending time with me, Mia. I hope we can do it again soon. Have a wonderful birthday party." Then she looked at Nora. "Thank you for the offer. It's very kind. I may take you up on it one of these days."

Callie held the door and watched them head to Nora's gold-colored sedan. After they left, Callie tossed Mia's plate in the trash, wiped paint off the counter where she'd had been sitting, then washed her hands. Returning to her stool, she reached for her brush. The water wash had dried, so she applied another light layer.

Her phone rang. She dried her hands on her jeans and reached for her cell. Wyatt's name showed on her screen.

"Hello?"

"Hey, Callie. It's Wyatt. Wanted to let you know I got ahold of Mom, and she'll be picking up Mia shortly."

"They just left, actually." She glanced toward the door, then set the phone on the counter and put it on speaker.

He exhaled. "Sorry. I meant to call sooner. I've been a little distracted."

"I hope everything's okay."

Wyatt didn't say anything for a moment. "My father-in-law broke his leg in two places. They were able to do X-rays here, but they need an orthopedic surgeon in Durango to do the surgery. Our small hospital isn't equipped for something like that."

Callie's hand stilled. "I'm sorry to hear that. Is there anything I can do to help in any way?"

"Caring for Mia was a great help. Thanks for offering, though it was last-minute."

"It wasn't a problem. I enjoyed spending time with her." He didn't need to know about his daughter's tears. "What can I do to help you?"

He didn't respond for a moment. "What do you mean?"

"With everything on your plate, how can I ease some of your burden? I don't know much about horses, but I'm a fast learner. I can help with feeding or brushing, or whatever else needs to be done."

As soon as the words left her mouth, she wanted to snatch back her offer. Too late.

She'd get used to their size, wouldn't she?

"Once I get a feel for the different activities at the guest ranch, I can lend more of a hand there as well. Or even with Mia, who is precious, by the way. I know you have your family and everything, but they seem busy too." Callie rehydrated the pans of color, loaded her brush with blue pigment, then applied it to her paper.

"Yeah, we're all busy. That's part of the problem."

"Then please let me help."

Again, another pause.

"Why would you do that? We're not your problems."

Callie rinsed her brush and let it sit on the edge of the cup. She moved off the chair and pushed through the screen door. She stepped onto the deck and pressed her back against the railing. "Because we're friends. Plus, my grandma would've been first in line to help her friends. Ray and Irene were so helpful when my grandma was sick. Now it's my turn to help them...and you. From what I've seen, you're pretty great at giving help but not so great at receiving it."

"How can I turn down such an offer? Tell you what—you mentioned needing renovations done on your gram's shop. I'll help you when I can, and I'll accept your help with the guest ranch, the horse rescue, or even with my daughter. How's that sound?"

"Sounds good to me. One more question."

"Shoot."

"How are you doing?" She lifted her face toward the early evening sun.

"I'm fine." His words came out in a rush.

"Are you?"

"I have to be. My in-laws need me."

"But what about what *you* need?"

"To be honest, Callie, I don't get asked that very often." He exhaled. "They're about to load Ray into the chopper, then I need to take Irene home. I'll touch base with you soon." He ended the call before she could say goodbye.

Callie stared at the screen and shook her head.

What was she doing? Acting so eager to step in and fix Wyatt's problems? Maybe because she couldn't manage her own chaos, it was easier to focus on someone else?

She didn't need any more complications right now. But she couldn't take it back. Instead, she'd work at being the kind of friend Wyatt needed.

And nothing more.

Chapter Three

Callie hadn't expected to spend the last morning of her very brief vacation heading into Aspen Ridge and stepping foot inside her gram's cottage.

It had been her favorite place as a child. And now, only memories kept her company.

Early morning sunshine filtered through the dusty stained glass window, throwing a prism of color across the dull wooden floor that needed a good polish to restore the shine.

Callie trailed a finger through the dust blanketing the empty display tables and high counter that held the register and doubled as Gram's desk. She pinched a cobweb strung from corner to corner of a wrought iron stand that used to hold handmade jewelry.

Music had always played in the background of the small shop that featured handmade products from local artists. Now only the sounds of Callie's flip-flops against the wooden floor disturbed the quiet.

As she scanned the walls that needed to be

scrubbed and refreshed with a bright coat of paint, Callie's eyes landed on a photo behind the cash register. She headed around the counter and lifted the frame off the sun-bleached wall, leaving behind a darker rectangle.

She traced a finger over the picture of Gram with her arm draped over Callie's shoulders. They held up ribbons they'd won at the art show they'd entered together—Callie with her first watercolor painting at the age of nine and Gram with her intricate and beautiful stained glass.

That was the moment Callie had realized she wanted to be an artist, and Gram had encouraged that dream until the day she died.

Her phone rang, signaling a video call. Callie pulled it out of her pocket and answered. "Hey, Mom."

"Hi, sweetheart. I tried to call last night, but you didn't answer. Figured you were busy getting settled at the guest ranch." Mom's phone bounced as she walked through what appeared to be some sort of outdoor market. Sunglasses shaded her eyes and her hair—the same dark color as Callie's—had been pulled back into a ponytail, highlighting her high cheekbones.

At fifty-two, her mother looked more like her older sister. A compliment that always pleased her.

Callie brushed off a wooden bench by the

front door and sat. "Yeah, sorry about that—I had a busy day and went to bed earlier than expected. I'm in Aspen Ridge right now."

"Doing what? You're supposed to be relaxing."

"I was. In fact, I started a new watercolor yesterday and plan to explore the area a little this afternoon. Now I'm checking out Gram's shop." Callie turned the phone and gave her a quick scan of the room, then turned it back to face her.

"I'm sure that's not easy." Mom cocked her head.

"Not really, but I can't put it off if I'm going to reopen the shop."

"Are you sure that's the best choice? Teaching is a much more stable profession, you know. You could always sell the cottage and use the money to pay off your student loans. Or use it for something more practical, like a down payment on a house."

Practical was her mother's middle name.

"I promised Gram, remember? She left me the shop for a reason, and I can't walk away without even trying. You and Dad taught me that. It's your fault for instilling a sense of integrity in the boys and me."

Mom sighed. A little too loudly. "Yes, we did. But what will you do for product?"

"I'll contact the artists who used to sell here

and see if they're interested once I bring the shop back to its former glory."

"You have a long way to go before that could happen."

"I'm aware." The to-do list growing in her head pressed on her shoulders. "But I have the whole summer to move in the right direction. I'll figure out how to come up with the money and make it happen."

She needed to be sure her move to Aspen Ridge wasn't going to cost her more than she could afford. Both in her wallet and in her already wounded heart.

"Since you won't take money from your dad and me, you could consider a short-term business loan so you can get the repairs done sooner. Then you can see if the shop is worth reopening or selling."

"That's an option." But not one she really wanted to take if she could help it. Her student loans were enough debt right now.

"Have you read the letter yet?"

Callie bit her lower lip and shook her head. "I can't."

Aaron Brewster, Gram's attorney, had given her family members letters Gram had written before she passed. Callie still had hers tucked away in Gram's bookcase upstairs. Unopened.

"You will when you're ready. Okay, I won't

take up any more of your time. I'm walking into church, but I wanted to see how you're doing. Love you, sweetie." Mom pressed two fingers to her own lips, then touched them to her screen.

"Thanks for calling, Mom. Love you too. Give Dad a hug. I'll check in soon." Callie ended the call and blew out a breath.

Her mother meant well and wanted only the best for Callie and her brothers, but a little encouragement would go a long way.

She was tired of living her life according to others' expectations. So, yes, Callie needed to get the shop reopened.

Somehow.

She headed for the back stairs that led to Gram's small apartment, where Callie would be living once her time at the guest ranch came to an end.

But as she put her foot on the bottom step, she lost all energy to keep climbing.

She wasn't ready to go upstairs where Gram's scent lingered. When her family was there after the funeral, Mom wanted to box up Gram's things, but Callie had talked her out of it.

It felt too soon to get rid of the neatly made bed, the knitted afghan thrown over the back of the couch, or even the translucent blue cup Gram used every morning for her first cup of tea.

She wasn't able to do it today either.

But eventually she'd have to find the strength to dive in so she could keep her promise.

As she moved off the bottom stair, she stepped on something. She bent down and pulled out a white piece of glass wedged under the wood.

But it wasn't just glass.

She retrieved a small stained glass dove with a sprig in its mouth.

Covered in dirt, the tiny bird appeared abandoned. Discarded. Unwanted.

She could relate.

Callie rubbed the smudges off the bird's wings. She'd take the bird back to the cabin, search the cataloged remaining inventory on her computer and try to find the rightful owner.

Releasing a deep sigh, she pulled her sunglasses off the top of her head, slid them onto her face and left the shop, locking the door behind her.

She lifted her face to the sunshine and pulled in a lungful of air.

Next door to Gram's cottage, barking echoed from inside the Aspen Ridge Animal Shelter, which was owned by Ray and Irene Douglas, Wyatt's in-laws. Painted barn red with black shutters, the shelter was a part of the Douglases' horse farm. Very few cars drove down the unlined road, which was on the outskirts of town.

Other than the barking, the only sounds were

the wind chimes hanging from the Douglases' front porch and blowing in the light breeze that brought up scents from the pasture.

The back door to the animal shelter opened. Wyatt stepped outside and closed the door behind him.

Dressed in tan slacks, a light blue button-down shirt open at the throat that highlighted his tanned skin, shined boots, and the same sunglasses he had on yesterday, Wyatt smiled. "Hey, Callie. I'm surprised to find you in town."

"Gavin Copeland came out last night and got me so I'd have my car. I was surprised he'd fixed it so quickly, but he was able to find a new alternator and get it installed yesterday afternoon. Said he didn't want to leave me stranded. This morning, I decided to head into town for breakfast, passed Gram's cottage and made an impromptu decision to check out the shop."

"Gavin's a good guy." He nodded toward the worn blue cottage. "How'd your visit go?"

Her fingers tightened around the stained glass dove. "Bittersweet."

"I get it. Been there. Sorry you have to go through that." His voice softened, and the tender tone nearly undid her.

She swallowed and cleared her throat. "What are you up to?"

Wyatt jerked his head toward the shelter. "I

stopped by to feed the animals. Ray had his surgery last night, and Irene spent the night in Durango with him, but she'll be back this afternoon."

"How's he doing?"

"He's in a little pain and tired. Didn't sleep much. His limited mobility is making him cranky. I talked with Irene, and I'll be handling the horse rescue."

"My offer to help still stands. Gram and Irene were good friends. I believe Gram bought her cottage from them after my grandfather passed away."

"Right—it used to belong to Irene's mother. Irene was pretty broken up over Ada's death. So, you're definitely reopening her shop?"

Callie dragged a hand through her hair. "When I stopped in, I planned to make a list of what needed to be done. But now I just don't know."

"Know about what?"

"It was tough walking inside this morning. Everything needs to be scrubbed down and repainted. The front porch needs fixing. Gram kept putting it off, then she had her stroke. I need to be able to stay longer than ten minutes if I'm going to get it reopened."

"Grief is tough. You can't rush it. Just walk through it." He removed his sunglasses and slid them into his front pocket. "Elbow grease is free, and I could give you a hand with painting. I know some guys who will fix the porch for you."

Callie settled a hand on her hip. "You're so kind to offer, but when will you have time? Your plate is nearly overflowing with responsibilities already."

He lifted a shoulder. "I like to keep busy. To help out where I can. To give back."

"That's sweet, but you don't owe me anything. There's nothing to give back. If anything, I owe you for yesterday. Not to mention all the help you gave Gram. She appreciated your family very much."

"If it weren't for your grandmother, I wouldn't have asked Linnea to marry me." He twisted his wedding band.

"I didn't know that. Gram never mentioned it."

"I had just enlisted and was heading off to boot camp. Linnea and I had talked about our futures since she was going off to college. And we ended up in a fight. I'd gone to the diner and found your grandma sitting there. She asked why I looked so sad and I spilled my guts."

"Gram had that effect on people."

"She was a great listener. After I told her what was going on, she looked at me and said, 'Wyatt, if you want to hold on to that girl, marry her.' I wasn't expecting to get engaged at eighteen, but

Linnea and I had been together since ninth grade and I knew she was the one for me."

"So, you proposed?"

"Well, it wasn't quite that easy. I had to go through her dad first and he was a tough nut to crack. We talked and decided it would be best for me to get through boot camp, and then when I took leave before my next duty station, we'd see where we were in our relationship. If we could handle three months apart with limited communication, then maybe we could handle the tough stuff too. But enough about me." His eyes drifted to her hand and his eyebrows knitted together. "What do you have there?"

"Oh, this." She lifted it to show him. "As I was leaving the shop, I found it wedged under the corner of the staircase. I pulled it out and was surprised to see it was intact. I decided to take it to the yurt and try to find the owner."

He moved closer and took it gently from her. "When I graduated from boot camp, your grandma gave me one just like it. Apparently, she'd taught a class on making them, so it's probably hers. Several ladies, including my mom and Irene, made them. It's probably kind of silly that a grown man would keep something like that, but she told me it symbolized hope. When things weren't going well, or I was getting deployed,

I kept it around, I guess, as a reminder to hold on to hope."

Fresh tears filled Callie's eyes. She really needed to get a grip on her emotions. She swallowed hard, then nodded. "Gram was great for holding on to hope."

Wyatt rubbed the back of his head. "Hey, not to change the subject, but I planned to stop by the guest ranch and run something by you. Since you're here, do you have a minute?"

She glanced at his clothes. "You look dressed for church. Sure you have time?"

"Actually, I hit the early service, then ducked out. Everly is teaching children's church today and promised to care for Mia so I could take care of things at the shelter for Ray and Irene."

The man was practically perfect.

If she were looking, he'd be the right kind of guy for her. But she wasn't looking. Love didn't last and led only to heartbreak. No, thank you.

"I probably should've gone. I thought about it, but I haven't been there since Gram's funeral." Arms folded over her chest, she turned and faced the road. The tip of the white steeple could be seen against the horizon. She faced Wyatt. "I'm not mad at God or anything like it. It's just…"

"You still see her sitting in that middle pew, don't you?"

Her head jerked up. "How'd you know?"

He shoved a hand in his front pocket and kicked a toe against the weathered railing. "When I came back home, it took me a while to sit in the same sanctuary where I got married."

She shook her head. "Grief is weird."

"Definitely." He held out a closed fist.

She bumped her knuckles against his. "What did you want to run by me?"

He handed the dove back to her. "You're welcome to stay in the yurt since you paid for it already. But if you'd like to spend this coming week training with Macey and me, then we're willing to refund your rental fee. You could move into the staff suites upstairs in the lodge." He nodded at the cottage. "Or stay here, if you wanted to commute. Our guests are scheduled to arrive this afternoon, so we'd have to move you soon."

She worked out the numbers quickly in her head. Putting the money back into her dwindling bank account would help.

She nodded. "Last night in the yurt was fun, but I could use the extra funds toward repairing the shop. Staff housing would be better. Gram's apartment isn't ready for me to move into just yet."

Neither was her heart.

One side of his mouth lifted in a lazy, Sunday morning way. "Not a problem at all. I'm sure you saw the suites when Mom gave you a tour of the lodge yesterday. You're our first staff member outside of family, but we built it hoping for continued growth. I need to head back to my place and change, so how about if I catch up with you in an hour or so?"

"Sounds good. See you then." She waved.

As Wyatt opened the door to his SUV, Callie fingered the textured milky glass one more time, then looked back at the cottage in need of a fresh coat of paint.

Maybe she needed to hold on to hope just a little longer and see where it took her.

One thing at a time.

Wyatt repeated his father's favorite mantra as he pulled into the graveled parking space in front of Callie's yurt.

Now that he'd taken care of things at the animal shelter for Ray and Irene, he could focus on getting Callie settled, then get ready for the arrival of their guests.

Then he could relax.

Right. Until something else—or someone else—needed his attention. But he wasn't about to begrudge the busyness.

It kept his mind occupied and didn't leave a lot of time for thinking, for longing, for missing what he should've had but didn't.

As he cut the engine, he spied someone sitting in one of the chairs at the end of the dock.

Callie.

He strode down the path that led to the water.

She twisted in her chair and waved. She set some sort of tray on the floor of the dock, then stood and faced him. "Hi, again."

He strode down the dock, his worn boots thudding against the new wood. "Hope I'm not intruding."

Shaking her head, she pushed her sunglasses on top of her head. "Not at all."

She wore the same green T-shirt and a pair of denim shorts from when he'd seen her in town. And bare feet. Her flip-flops had been kicked to the side. Her dark brown hair had been gathered in the same sort of messy knot that his sisters favored.

And the sight of her made his heart thump wildly in his chest.

What was *that* about?

At the end of the dock, he stretched out his arms and inhaled, breathing in the scents of the lake.

The sun hovered over the treetops, spilling liquid gold over the darkened water. A family of ducks flapped and landed on the glassy surface and sent ripples toward the shore.

"It's easy to get lost in the beauty, isn't it?"

Callie's words came out in nearly a whisper as if she were afraid to disturb the tranquility.

"Best place on earth, in my opinion."

"I can see why." She lifted a large sheet of paper off the tray and held it out to him. "Paint can't capture the essence, but I've been trying."

He took it and found splashes of color gliding across the thick paper as the landscape in front of him came to life in a watercolor haze. He shook his head, then looked at her. "Callie, this is incredible. You're underestimating yourself."

She shrugged and reached for it. "First time I painted since Gram died. Started it yesterday while caring for Mia. When I returned from town, the water beckoned so I decided to paint for a while."

"Until I interrupted."

She shook her head and shot him a smile. "I'm glad you did."

Spoken quietly, the four words quickened his pulse.

What was his problem?

"Ready to get moved into the lodge, or would you rather do more painting?"

"I can paint later. I didn't do much unpacking, so moving my things won't take much time." She reached for a tray that held a metal rectangular tin, a few brushes, a worn towel with splashes of color, and a disposable cup of murky water.

"Here, I'll take that." He took the tray from her as she reached for her pad of paper and the loose sheet she'd been painting.

As they headed back, she sidestepped an exposed tree root, and her shoulder brushed his.

At the yurt, he reached for the door, then followed her inside. He set the tray on the island. She gathered brushes, paints and a pad of paper off the counter and tucked them in her black, zippered case.

She moved to the fridge and retrieved a paper covered in paint, then handed it to him. "Mia painted this yesterday while I cared for her."

He took it and smiled. "Cute. She talked about you all night and wanted to know when she could paint with 'that lady' again. Feel free to add any art activities to the daily schedule."

"I'd like that." Callie wheeled her suitcase across the floor, flung her art case over her shoulder and picked up her purse off the table by the door. "All set. I'll drop my things off at the lodge, then come back and clean up."

"No need. Everly will go through it after church. We have a couple of families on our waiting list, so we'll see if they're still interested in renting it this week."

"But it's my mess. She's not responsible for cleaning up after me. She's busy enough. I don't mind."

"If you're sure, then I'll let her know. Macey plans to meet with you after lunch, if you have time, to review what will happen this afternoon."

She spread out her arms, her grin just as wide. "All I have right now is time. I do plan to make another quick trip into town before the guests arrive and make an actual to-do list of what needs to be done at the shop. I kind of rushed through it this morning."

"If you want to go after we move your things into the lodge, I'll be free for a couple of hours." He reached for the handle of her suitcase and wheeled it onto the deck.

Callie followed and closed the door behind them. "That's a luxury for you. Don't waste it going through dusty rooms. Take time for yourself."

"I'm not sure how to do that anymore."

"Exactly. Sounds like you need to learn."

Wyatt dug out his keys, found the one for the lodge, then unlocked the main door. He pushed it open, then stepped back for Callie to pass.

As she moved into the expansive room, a light citrus scent floated past him.

Scents of wood and lemon oil mingled with the pork roasting in the slow cookers that Mom had filled before leaving for church.

He nodded toward the stairs. "I'll show you to your room."

Upstairs, Wyatt stopped in the middle of the

loft and waved his hand toward several closed doors. "You have your choice of suites. They're all pretty much the same—queen beds, love seat and desk, private bathroom and a kitchenette. You're welcome to join us for all meals, but if you need a break, you can bring food up here or make something yourself."

Callie moved past him and turned in a semi-circle. She headed toward the room that faced the water, turned the handle and stepped inside.

Shards of light sprawled across the bed covered with a quilt done in blues, purples and reds. A wooden rocker sat in one corner. In the opposite corner, a love seat and a small workstation took up the space. A four-drawer dresser stood against the wall across from the bed. Next to it, a microwave sat on a stand with a dorm fridge tucked in underneath.

"It's lovely."

"I'm glad you like it." He wheeled her suitcase in front of the closed bathroom door. "I'll leave you alone so you can unpack. The offer still stands if you'd like help when you head into town."

She pulled out her phone and glanced at the screen. "I can unpack later. I'll take advantage of the time I have now and head back into town."

"I can drive, if you'd like. Or would you like to take two vehicles?"

She eyed him a moment then shook her head.

"Wyatt, you're so kind to offer, but I get the sense you don't have a lot of downtime."

He shrugged. "There's always something to be done or someone who needs help."

"Exactly. And I don't want to add to your incredibly long to-do list, even though I truly appreciate your offer. Besides, you're my employer now. How would it look?"

"Look? To whom? I'm simply a guy helping a friend. Nothing more."

It would stay that way. Keeping his distance was best for the both of them.

"Besides, didn't you offer to help me out too? It's an exchange of services."

She paused a moment, then nodded, although her shoulders remained tense as she brushed past him and headed down the stairs.

Five minutes later, they headed into town with the windows down and radio turned up to hear over the wind.

Callie settled into the passenger seat, her fingers drumming to the beat against her knee. Maybe now she'd relax a little.

He pulled into the driveway between the cottage and the animal shelter and cut the engine.

Callie didn't wait for him to open her door. She scrambled out and headed for the small back porch. She unlocked the back door and stepped inside the cottage.

And stopped so quickly he nearly ran into her. He grabbed her arms to keep from plowing her over. "You okay?"

She nodded but didn't turn around. "Her scent gets me every time. It's everywhere."

He understood all too well. Unfortunately.

He released her arms and scrubbed a hand over his face. "After my wife died, Mia and I slept on a buddy's couch for a month because I couldn't stand to be in our apartment. He took my keys, went to my place and packed enough things for Mia and me so I didn't have to deal with it."

She turned and looked at him, her eyes large and glistening. She lifted a hand toward his face, then dropped it before she made contact. "Thank you for sharing that. I'm so sorry you had to suffer such a loss."

She dropped her purse on a small table inside the door, took two steps forward, then wrapped her arms around her stomach, facing him once again. "How am I going to get the shop fixed up if walking inside is such a big deal?"

"The same way I did—one day at a time. Some days will be easier than others."

She nodded and took a few more steps into the room. She squared her shoulders then strode behind the counter. She ducked down then stood with a yellow legal pad and a pen in her hand.

"Enough dillydallying, as Gram would say. It's time to make a plan."

Despite the shimmering in her eyes, her smile showed she wouldn't let her grief defeat her.

He rubbed his hands together and joined her at the counter. "Okay, what's first?"

Tapping the pen against her chin, she moved around him and stood in the middle of the room, slowly turning in a circle as if appraising everything. "Everything needs to be removed from this room. The walls need scrubbed and repainted. Windows need to be washed and new shades or coverings put up. The floor needs refinishing. I think that will be a good start."

"I agree." He jerked a thumb over his shoulder. "I'll head next door and see if Irene has boxes that haven't been broken down for recycling yet. We can begin taking things off the walls and clearing the room today."

"That sounds great. Thanks." She shot him another smile that caused his gut to tighten.

Behind them, someone rapped on the back door.

He turned and found his mother-in-law standing on the back porch, a foil-covered plate in her hands.

He crossed the room and opened the door. "Hey, Mama D. When did you get back?"

"About an hour ago. Ray's napping. I saw your

SUV but you weren't in the house. Then I saw the lights on in the cottage and figured Callie was here."

"Yes, she is. I came to give her a hand before we have to head back to the ranch. Come in."

He stepped aside and held the door open. "Callie, you have a visitor. Remember my mother-in-law, Irene Douglas?"

Irene's kind blue eyes softened as Callie approached with her arms outstretched. "Of course. It's great to see you again, Irene."

"Hi, Callie. It's good to see you again too. Ada was a dear friend, and I miss her every day."

Callie nodded, understanding that feeling well.

Irene thrust a plate at her. "I just made a batch of brownies and wanted to share."

Callie took the plate and peeled back a corner of the foil, releasing the scent of sugar and chocolate. "Thanks, they smell great. Sorry to hear about Ray's fall and surgery. Please let me know if there's anything I can do to help."

Irene's eyes lowered, then she gave Callie a small smile. "Thanks. Right now, we're trusting the Lord for his healing. So prayers would be greatly appreciated."

"Of course."

Irene reached for the door handle. "I'll get out of your hair. Wyatt, got a minute?"

He followed Irene outside and down the steps. She paused at the driveway and faced him, a wide smile across her face. "Callie's a great girl. Ada adored her, you know."

Nodding, he stuffed his hands in his pockets, sensing he wasn't about to like what she said next. "Don't you think it's time to get back on the horse, as they say?"

He didn't know who *they* were, but he wasn't interested in what they had to say.

He slung an arm over the woman's shoulders and steered her toward her own back porch. "Mama D, I appreciate the advice, but I'm not interested in dating. I'll never find someone like Linnea."

"Oh, honey." She turned and pressed a hand against his cheek. "I know that more than anyone. My daughter was one of a kind. But don't look for her clone. Find someone who makes you happy. That's what she'd want for you. She wouldn't want you to spend the rest of your life alone. And Mia needs a mother."

He wrapped his fingers around her small hand and gave it a gentle squeeze. "I am happy. Besides, Mia has you, my mom and my sisters. She's not lacking for strong role models. She's one blessed little girl."

"Don't allow the pain of your past to dictate your future. That's all I'm saying."

Despite her words, that wouldn't be the last thing she said on the subject. She'd been hinting for a while that it was time for him to move on.

While Wyatt appreciated his mother-in-law's advice—and anyone else with an opinion about his future—she didn't get it.

She understood grief and the pain of losing a child, which no parent should have to endure, but she hadn't lost the love of her life.

Opening his heart again meant exposing himself to future heartache, and he definitely wasn't going to do that again.

No matter what anyone said.

Chapter Four

Callie just needed to get through the next hour.

She didn't need to learn everything about managing the guest ranch in one day. Macey had promised to be by her side all week long and answer any questions she had.

Would one week be enough?

While they moved everything out of Gram's shop and took everything off the walls, Wyatt had asked if she was ready for the challenge of managing the guest ranch.

She'd said yes, hoping her voice was stronger than her nervous stomach.

Had she taken on more than she could handle? She never second-guessed herself like this, even when she was doing student teaching or finding her way through her first year.

But she'd figure it out, like she always did when faced with new situations. She didn't want to let Wyatt down and have him regret hiring her due to her lack of experience.

She needed to get a grip, or it was going to be a very long summer.

In the last hour, two different families had arrived in minivans as well as a young couple who showed up in a vintage bright yellow VW Beetle that her grandma would've loved.

The serenity of the guest ranch had been shattered by slamming doors, laughing children and adult voices.

And the Stone family took it in stride.

To them, registration meant all hands on deck.

Wyatt's older brother, Bear, and Macey's husband, Cole, helped outside while Piper, Bear's wife, stayed in the lodge with Callie and Macey and directed the families to their correct yurts.

Everly kept the younger children engaged with bubbles and sidewalk chalk while their parents unloaded their vehicles.

Deacon and Nora worked in the kitchen, preparing a welcome dinner of pulled pork, baked beans, potato salad, tossed salad and several kinds of pies.

The scents wafting throughout the lodge made Callie's stomach growl even louder. She pressed a hand against her abdomen, hoping no one else heard. She hadn't eaten anything other than coffee and one of Irene's brownies.

Maybe some water would help.

She searched for her bottle, but it wasn't on

the registration table. She must've left it on one of the picnic tables outside.

She turned to Macey, who kept her cool through the very busy hour. "I'm going to grab my water. I'll be right back."

"No problem." Macey smiled at her as the baby napped in her arms.

As Callie left the air-conditioned lodge, the sticky heat smacked her in the face. Humidity hung in the air as dark clouds rolled across the sky. A storm was coming. Hopefully, it would hold off until everyone had gotten settled in their yurts for the night.

She found her now-warm water bottle sitting where she'd left it on the picnic table. As she turned to return to the lodge, something fluffy and white streaked past her and raced for the water.

"Fewix, come back." A boy, a little younger than Mia maybe, ran between the two yurts on Callie's left side and toddled after the dog.

Callie waited a second for an adult to emerge, but no one appeared. Everly had gone inside right before Callie left, but where were the guys?

The dog stopped at the end of the dock next to one of the Adirondack chairs and barked, its tail wagging. The little boy with dark curls ran toward it with chubby, outstretched arms.

Oh, that wasn't going to end well.

Callie ran down the path, praying she'd reach him before he could fall in. As she reached the dock, someone stepped off the path that wound along the water.

They collided and something smacked against the ground. Dressed in black, the person wasn't much taller than she was. A teen maybe? Not taking the time to stop and check, Callie called over her shoulder. "Sorry!"

"Hey, you broke my..." The person's words carried in the wind as Callie's feet pounded against the wood.

The little boy tried to grab the dog, but it spun quickly. Its backside hit the child's legs, buckling his knees. The child pitched forward head-first into the water.

"Nooo!" The words, ripped from Callie's throat, echoed across the lake. Dropping her water bottle, she dove into the water. She surfaced, pushed the hair out of her eyes and searched frantically for the little boy.

He flailed just a few feet in front of her, crying and choking. Then he went under again.

Callie's blood turned to ice. She dove back under and made out the hazy red of his shorts in the murky lake water stirred up from the activity. She caught him around the waist and hauled him to her chest. She kicked hard and pushed to the surface.

Choking, the little boy sobbed and clung to Callie's neck so tightly she struggled to fill her burning lungs with air. She tried to loosen the tight grip he had on her throat.

Footsteps thundered down the dock. A large splash on the other side of her threw water in their faces. Treading water, Callie turned and held the little boy against her chest, using her shoulder to protect him against the blast.

She wiped her face again and found Wyatt swimming toward her. He dragged a hand across his face. "Hey, you okay?"

She nodded, her teeth starting to chatter.

"Callie, give him to me."

She turned and found Bear kneeling at the end of the dock with his arms stretched out. Another man with his face twisted in anguish knelt beside him.

With her own arms feeling like icicles, she lifted the child up with as much strength as she could.

Bear reached for him, but as he grabbed him, Callie's hands slipped off the little boy's wet skin.

Losing her balance, she fell forward and grazed the top of her head on the edge of the dock. She went back under, water shooting up her nose.

Wyatt wrapped a strong arm around her and

pulled her against him. She surfaced once again, coughing.

Teeth chattering, she shivered as the adrenaline drained from her body. She clung to Wyatt as she caught her breath.

"Think you can climb back onto the dock?"

Suddenly aware of just how close he was and how tightly she'd been holding on to him, she nodded.

With her forehead burning, head aching, and body turning to jelly, she forced herself to move out of his strong arms. She swam a few strokes to the ladder attached to the side of the dock and pulled herself out of the water.

She wanted nothing more than to collapse on the wood.

Clapping ricocheted across the lake, jerking her attention to the crowd gathered on the dock.

Heat seared her face.

The man who had knelt next to Bear hugged the little boy close. A woman raced toward them and wrapped a blanket around them.

Turning to Callie and with tears streaking her makeup, she threw her arms around her. "Thank you for saving my son. I tried to get Teddy into the yurt and didn't realize our dog Felix had run outside. I'm so sorry for the trouble we've caused, but I'm so thankful you were there."

Trying not to shiver, Callie shook her head.

"I'm just grateful he's okay. You should get him checked out to be sure there are no injuries."

With a nod, the woman returned to the man holding the soaked little boy and they headed back up the dock.

As she wrapped her arms over her chest and rubbed her skin to generate some warmth, Callie's eyes drifted to Deacon and Nora talking to a man who didn't look pleased standing next to the person in black, who Callie could now see was a male teen.

The kid turned and pointed at her.

Macey rushed past them and wrapped a fleece blanket around Callie. "Take this so you can warm up."

Callie burrowed in it and tucked her fists under her jaw as she tried to calm her chattering teeth. "Who's that kid?"

"The son of one of our guests. Apparently, he was searching for a signal for his phone and claims you pushed him. His phone fell against a rock and shattered the screen."

"I didn't push him on purpose. I was running for the dock and ran into him. I'll pay to have his phone fixed." She did a mental calculation, knowing the cost was going to take money from her dwindling savings.

Macey slid an arm around Callie's shoulders. "The only thing you're going to do is take a shower. Then we're going to the clinic to get your head checked out."

Callie had forgotten about her injury. She touched her forehead. She couldn't tell if the moisture was lake water or blood. "It's fine. Just a graze."

Macey eyed her. "I'd feel better knowing you didn't have a mild concussion."

"I appreciate it, Macey, but other than a scrape and maybe a bruise, I'll be fine. Truly. If I have a headache or anything, I'll let you know."

She walked barefoot across the warm wood. Her flip-flops must be floating in the lake since they hadn't stayed on her feet after she dove in to save Teddy.

Someone called her name. She closed her eyes and paused. She turned and found Wyatt jogging toward her, soaked and in socked feet. He must've kicked off his boots before plunging into the water. His gray T-shirt clung to his brawny chest like a second skin.

He caught up to them and framed her face in his cold hands. His eyebrows scrunched together as he touched her wound gently. Then he glanced at his sister. "Can you take her in to get this checked?"

"That's what I was trying to talk her into doing. She claims she's fine." Macey raised an eyebrow. "Sounds like someone else I know."

Wyatt laughed, and the timbre of his voice warmed Callie's numb insides. Then he looked at Callie with a more serious expression. "Other than your forehead, are you sure you're okay?"

She nodded, not wanting him to release her.

He flashed her a smile and wrapped his arm around her shoulders, giving her a quick squeeze. "Good. Can't lose my best employee on her first day."

"You're not firing me?"

He released her and scowled. "Fire you? Why would I do that?"

She nodded to the teenager still standing on the dock with the man and Wyatt's parents. "Apparently, I broke that kid's phone."

Wyatt scoffed. "Phones can be replaced. If it weren't for you, we would've had a tragedy on our hands. Your quick thinking saved Teddy. You're a hero."

Callie's face heated under his watchful eyes and generous words. She shook her head. "Thank you. I just did what anyone else would've done."

"But you were the one who did it." He placed his hands on her blanket-covered shoulders, then rubbed her upper arms. "Get warmed up and into dry clothes. I really want you to get your head checked." Releasing her once again, he walked backward while pulling his keys from his sodden jeans pocket. "When I get back, we'll have dinner, then I need to head to Ray and Irene's to feed the animals."

Macey gave Callie's shoulder a squeeze. "You heard the boss. Get warm, and I'll take you to the clinic. On the way, I'll share what we have planned for the week. I promise not every day will be this adventurous."

As Callie entered the air-conditioned lodge and climbed the steps with rubbery legs, Macey's words echoed in her head.

Wyatt's sister was wrong.

To Callie, the adventure had just begun.

Working alongside Wyatt was going to test her in every way possible. She had a feeling he was going to be a distraction she didn't need. Was she up to the challenge of managing the guest ranch alongside him?

Only one way to find out.

What a way to kick off their new summer season.

Wyatt didn't even want to think about what would've happened if Callie hadn't acted so quickly.

After he returned to the guest ranch in dry clothes, he, Dad, Bear and Cole had a quick discussion about adding a gate and fence in front of the dock. While it may ruin the aesthetic, they needed to prevent another situation like this afternoon's mishap and protect their youngest guests.

At least Callie had agreed to get her head checked and allowed Macey to take her.

When Mia overheard him tell his parents that Ray had been released from the hospital, she begged to go with him so she could visit Grammy and Pappy and give him a kiss so he would get better.

How could he say no to that?

After a quick call to Irene, he now stood on their back porch, holding Mia's hand. He needed to leave her with Irene so he could get the animals fed and turned out.

Wyatt rapped two knuckles on the side door that led into Ray and Irene's kitchen. Then he opened it and stepped inside. "Mama D? You here?"

"Come on in, Wyatt. I'll be down in a minute."

Releasing his hand, Mia ran into the kitchen, then stopped. She cupped her small hands around her mouth. "Pappy, where are you? I wanna give you a kiss to make you better."

"In here, Peanut." Wyatt's father-in-law called from the living room, his deep voice threaded with fatigue.

Mia raced through the dining room and the open French doors that led into the living room.

From his spot by the sink, Wyatt watched as

she hurried to the couch where Ray lay reclined, his left leg in a cast and propped on pillows.

Mia knelt beside him, kissed his cheek and pressed her hand against the older man's forehead. He wrapped an arm around her and hauled her to his chest.

Turning away to give them privacy, Wyatt faced the window over the sink that gave a gorgeous view of the horse rescue.

A pair of recently rescued, underfed palominos grazed in the grass. They swished away flies with their tails that needed a good brushing, as the evening sun turned their gold coats nearly white.

They should've been brought in and fed a while ago. Wyatt should've gotten there sooner, but with the chaos at the guest ranch, things had taken longer than he'd expected.

He scanned the fence line and noticed a sagging post. That would need to be shored up so horses didn't find an escape route.

The weight of his new responsibilities pressed on him, but he'd find his rhythm and get a schedule worked out so he could manage his responsibilities.

He had to.

"Okay, sorry about that. I was getting bedding from the upstairs linen closet to make a bed for Ray in the guest room. He won't be able to climb stairs for a while." Irene came into the kitchen carrying a loaded laundry basket. Her hair had been pulled back into a low ponytail and she wore a white T-shirt and jean shorts. Dark circles shadowed her eyes. Apparently, she didn't get much sleep either.

"Let me get that for you." He took the basket and carried it into the guest room on the other side of the dining room. Seeing the queen-size mattress covered in only a pad, he made quick work of making up the bed. Instinct had him folding down the top sheet and blanket and tucking the edges tightly under the mattress.

He wasn't in the Marine Corps any longer, and no one would be inspecting his rack. He pulled the blanket out and smoothed out the sides.

As he returned to the kitchen, Mia streaked past him and climbed onto her booster seat attached to one of the wooden chairs that stayed at the table. "Grammy, do you have any brownies left?"

"Did someone say brownies?" Ray hobbled slowly into the kitchen, a little unsteady with the crutches. "Wyatt. How's it going?"

Dressed in his usual plaid Western shirt and a pair of shorts that exposed very pale legs, he appeared to be the same ole Ray Douglas Wyatt had known most of his life.

Except for the paleness beneath his tan and

the deep lines fanning out from reddened eyes darkened with circles.

Ray gripped the back of Mia's chair as he lowered himself onto the seat next to her. With hunched shoulders as if carrying the weight of the world, Ray appeared a decade older than fifty-eight.

"How are you doing, Ray?" Wyatt clamped a hand on his shoulder.

Ray glared at him, then raised an eyebrow. "About like a guy who just had his leg cut open."

"I'm sorry."

Ray waved away his words and rested his crutches against the table, but one toppled over and knocked to the floor. He muttered something under his breath and stretched out an arm for it.

"I got it." Wyatt picked it up and set it back against the table within Ray's reach. "Hey, I wanted to run something by you."

"What's on your mind, son?"

"I talked with Dad yesterday and wondered if you had a minute to talk? It can wait until after I do the feeding."

Ray lifted a hand and dropped it at his side. "Sure. I have at least six weeks of doing nothing. Plenty of time to talk. What's weighing you down?"

That was a loaded question.

Wyatt's gaze shifted between his in-laws.

As if reading his mind, Irene unbuckled Mia's booster seat. "Mia, let's go check on the kitties and make sure they have enough water before they go night-night."

Always excited to visit the animals in the shelter, Mia smiled and clapped her hands. "Okay, Grammy." She reached for Irene's hand.

Once the kitchen door closed behind them, Wyatt pulled out a chair and sat. He folded his arms on the table in front of him. "Yesterday, I offered to buy in as a partner. I could use—"

"What'd I tell you about that rumor?" Ray cut him off, his voice thundering in the quiet room.

Amazing how quickly the man could turn from doting Pappy to a crusty cowboy.

"I know money's tight right now, so don't even try to deny it. Partner with me, and you'll retain the ranch for good. You're out of commission until your leg heals anyway, and you need someone to look after things."

"I'll manage." Ray scrubbed a hand over his unshaven face.

Wyatt shook his head. "Trying to manage everything by yourself is what got you hurt in the first place. You're too stubborn to ask for help."

"Fine. I'll accept a hand for the time being as long as I can trust you to not to mess up what my family has worked so hard to establish. Happy?"

"You can trust me. You also know how much

Linnea loved the horses. If I buy it, then I'll turn it into a sanctuary so they're protected."

"That takes too much time and work. Not to mention money. And constant monitoring of the kill lots to find the right horses. We can't save them all."

"I get that. I wish we could." He stood, moved to the sink and filled a glass with water. "You once said you try to get them healthy, so they can be adopted by good families. And those fees help fund the rescue. But if we turned the rescue into a sanctuary, then we could apply for non-profit status and receive grants to cover costs. Plus, we could retrain those horses for a renewed purpose."

"Adopting a horse isn't as easy as picking out a cat or a dog." Ray jerked a thumb toward the barn. "Right now, I have ten malnourished or abused horses that need more love and care. They won't be eligible for adoption for a long time."

"Then let's consider monthly sponsorships—people who are willing to donate time and money for their care and feeding. In return, they can provide affection and gentle riding so the horses can get used to riders again."

"Son, your heart is in the right place, and I appreciate that, but my mind's made up."

Wyatt folded his arms over his chest and

schooled his tone. "A month ago, there was a big write-up in one of the magazines I read on-line about horses being sold for slaughter. As a sanctuary, we could stop that and offer them so much more."

"You don't give up, do you? If I become a non-profit, then I need to create a board, and I don't need other people telling me how to run my own ranch." He waved his hand toward the property. "I'm one guy, and I'd like to keep it that way."

His set jaw and raised brow told Wyatt he wasn't about to budge, and that Wyatt was wasting his breath trying.

He drained his water, then he lifted both hands, palms facing Ray. "All right. Fine. Just know the offer's still there. I'm heading to the barn. Once I'm done, I'll swing back for Mia. If you feel up to it, we can talk about what needs to be done this week, and I'll fit it into my schedule."

Ray straightened in his chair and puffed out his chest. "Of course I'll feel up to it. All I'm asking is for a hand. Think you can do that?"

Wyatt wouldn't let Ray's gruff tone get under his skin. He stuck out his hand. "Sure, Ray. Not a problem."

"Good. And stop carrying the world on your shoulders, Wy. Give those burdens over to the Lord, and let Him carry them for you."

Easier said than done.

As he headed to the barn, Wyatt longed to head back to the ranch. Maybe stretch out in front of the campfire that would be starting soon and relax for the night.

But that wasn't about to happen. Too much still needed to be done. Maybe if he could prove himself to Ray, then the older man would allow him to partner with the rescue and help ease some of his burden.

Didn't at least one of them deserve a break?

Chapter Five

What had Callie gotten herself into?

Why had she even offered to help with the horse rescue when the large animals intimidated her?

Because Wyatt was willing to give up his valuable time to help her at the shop. She wanted to do what she could to help him out in return... and to convince him he hadn't made a mistake in hiring her.

But could she do this? Really?

She'd have to. She'd given her word.

When Wyatt mentioned skipping tonight's campfire to head to Ray and Irene's to feed the horses before his meeting, she'd offered to lend a hand since she planned to wash walls in the shop anyway. She wanted to start painting tomorrow.

With the first part of the week having been so busy, she hadn't been in town since Macey took her to the clinic to get her head checked.

Inside the barn, the air swirled with dust

motes riding on bits of hay from bales being thrown down from upstairs. Wyatt jogged down the wooden steps and strode to the middle of the first floor where several bales toppled over one another.

"The hay separates into flakes, and each horse gets two flakes. We're not fancy around here, so it gets dropped into their stalls." He pitched hay over the stall door, then turned to her and waved a hand down the remaining stalls. "Do what I just did—break it apart and drop it in their stalls. While they're eating that, I'll mix their grain. We'll pour it into their feeders, rinse out their water buckets, refill them, then they'll be good to go."

He pushed to his feet and brushed dust and hay off his jeans. "When I return from my meeting and get Mia from Irene and Ray's, I'll turn them out and clean their stalls."

Mia twirled next to him, her sandaled feet making tracks in the dirt. "Daddy, can I feed the horsies too?"

"Sure thing, squirt. You can scoop the grain into the buckets, okay?"

Mia nodded and danced in a circle.

Oh, to have that kind of enthusiasm.

Callie broke apart the flakes as Wyatt had done, then eyed the stalls that came up to her shoulders.

The horses with their long muzzles and dark eyes watched her.

How was she supposed to get the hay in the stalls with them in the way?

Wyatt just dropped it in, but he'd been around the animals his whole life.

And these horses seemed more on edge than the calmer ones at Stone River.

On the way to the Douglas ranch, Wyatt had shared some of the conditions the horses had been in before Ray rescued them. Callie had to fight back tears against the inhumanity. Even now, some of them were still nothing more than skin and bones.

"What's the matter, Callie? You scared?"

Callie jumped at the sound of Mia's voice behind her.

Leave it to her to be so skittish that a child startled her.

Still holding an arm full of hay, Callie turned. "I'm not used to horses like you. How long have you been riding?"

Mia threw her arms out wide and rolled her eyes at Callie. "Like my whole life."

Callie bit her lip.

Right. Schooled by a three-year-old.

"The horsies just want some love. Right, Daddy?"

"Right, sweetheart." He carried a bucket and

set it in front of the stalls. Then he looked at Callie. "You okay?"

What could she say? That she was too afraid to throw hay into the stall?

Instead, she nodded and tossed the hay over the stall door as Wyatt had a moment ago. Except, she tossed it in the same stall. "Oops, sorry."

He grinned as he patted the brown horse's neck "No worries. Pearl won't mind. She can use the extra forage. She's being kept inside until her wounds heal."

Callie didn't even want to ask where they came from. Instead, she grabbed more flakes and carried them to the stall next to Pearl. A smaller whitish horse named Charlie nudged her arm.

"Daddy, can I pet Charlie?"

Wyatt lifted Mia in his arms and carried her to the horse's stall. He held on to the horse's harness while Mia rubbed her small hand over the black spot on the horse's head. "Charlie's a pony, and he's blind. We found him at a k-i-l-l lot a year ago. He's as gentle as can be and loves the attention. Mia adores him because of his size."

"How do you handle it?"

Wyatt didn't pretend not to understand her question. He lifted a shoulder. "Through the grace of God, I guess. What we see when we rescue these fine animals is enough to get the kindest, most patient person fired up."

Callie dropped the flakes over the pony's stall. As she reached out to rub Charlie's muzzle, he nudged her arm. She tried to move out of his way, and he nipped the tender flesh above her elbow.

"Ow!" She jumped back and twisted her arm.

Wyatt set Mia down and reached for Callie's elbow. "Did he nip you?"

"I think so. It doesn't really hurt. Just surprised me more than anything."

"Silly pony. Charlie, Callie's not food." Mia stood in front of the stall with her hands on her hips. "He doesn't know the difference between a nip and a nuzzle."

Wyatt ran a rough finger over the reddened spot. "I'm sorry. He doesn't usually do that. Maybe he thought you were sweet and wanted a taste."

Callie's eyes flew to Wyatt's face and found him grinning at her. But there was something else in his eyes. Something she couldn't quite decipher. Did she even want to try?

"Let me kiss it." Mia pulled on Callie's arm. "Grammy says kisses make everything better."

Callie crouched in front of the child and offered her arm. Mia brushed a light kiss across her skin. "There, how's that?"

Callie hugged Mia. "Thank you for making me feel better."

"You're welcome." She pressed a hand against Callie's cheek. "I like you."

Her heart nearly melting, Callie twirled one of Mia's pigtails around her finger. "I like you too, Mia."

"Can I help you throw the hay to the horsies?"

Callie glanced at Wyatt, and he nodded. "Mia, I'll pick you up. Callie will give you the hay, and you can throw it over the door. How's that?"

"Good idea, Daddy."

Wyatt scooped his daughter up, and Callie broke off more flakes for Mia. Since they all worked together, they were done in just a few minutes. Wyatt added grain to their feeders and refilled their water.

The horses shuffled their feet and lifted their heads when he approached their stalls. But when Mia came near them, they settled down.

"Mia's a little horse whisperer like you." Callie rested a shoulder against one of the empty stalls as she listened to Mia talking to Charlie again.

"I believe they sense her innocence and gentleness." Wyatt rested a hand against the stall above her head and searched her face. "I wish you'd told me the horses still made you nervous. I would've fed them."

His quiet words and lack of judgment still caused her face to warm. "I didn't want to go back on my word. You've been helping me so much this week, I wanted to return the favor. And I didn't want you to think you'd made a mistake in hiring me."

"Callie, no one's keeping score. You're more of a help than you know. Hiring you was one of the best decisions I've made in a while. You've been a pro this week. We'll work on getting you more comfortable with the horses, but no pressure." He shot her a smile that tripped her pulse, then looked at his watch. "I need to take Mia into the farmhouse, then get to my meeting. I'll see you back at the guest ranch?"

"Thanks." His words brought her more comfort than she was willing to confess. "I'm heading to the shop for a while. I want to get the walls washed down, then I'll call it a night."

"If you're still planning to paint tomorrow, I'll give you a hand."

Not trusting her voice at the moment, she nodded and followed him outside. Mia ran across the grass and disappeared into her grandparents' house. Callie cut across to the shop.

As she unlocked the back door, she replayed Mia's reactions to the animals. Callie longed to have that kind of confidence and peace.

And Wyatt's reassuring words did more than

dispel her fears. They reminded her of her priorities—her job and getting the shop reopened.

She couldn't get sidetracked by anything else, including a very handsome cowboy and his adorable daughter.

Wyatt was late to his own meeting, but he had no one to blame but himself.

He'd spent too much time with Callie, then ended up talking with Ray longer than expected when he dropped Mia off with her grandparents.

The time with Callie had him wishing he didn't have to leave. He didn't like the way they'd left things. He felt like a jerk for not seeing her nervousness around the horses. The last thing he wanted was to make her uncomfortable anywhere on the ranch.

If only she'd gone with him a different night. Part of him wished he could cancel the support group, but that wasn't possible since he was the leader of the motley crew of fathers.

Usually, he looked forward to seeing the guys who'd become like family. They understood each other's struggles, and it was a safe place to vent, when necessary.

At the church, he parked his SUV and stepped out into the muggy evening air. Even though the sun was lower in the sky, the heat hadn't leveled off yet.

Sweat slicked his forehead by the time he reached the back door. He took the carpeted stairs two at a time down to the basement where a dozen single fathers waited to discuss their dating and parenting struggles in one of the adult Sunday school rooms.

The rich scent of freshly brewed coffee floated up the steps, reminding him he'd forgotten to stop at the diner for whatever weekly treat Lynetta liked to send to spoil the men.

He'd been too focused on meeting Callie at the ranch. More like just too focused on Callie.

As he passed the open door that led to the pastor's office, a familiar laugh stopped him in his tracks.

Callie?

What was she doing there?

As he tried to peek discreetly around the corner, she turned and caught him. Her eyes widened as she cocked her head. "Wyatt? What are you doing here?"

Busted.

He jerked a thumb over his shoulder toward the lit room across the hall. "My meeting is here. I oversee a support group for single fathers. What about you?"

She shook her head and reached behind him, tugging on the back of his T-shirt.

"What's wrong?"

"Nothing. Just checking to see where you keep your cape. You're like some sort of Superman. Is there anything you can't do?"

He laughed softly and shook his head as heat crawled up his neck. "There's a lot I can't do. Thankfully, I have people in my corner like you who pick up the slack. What are you doing here?"

"I found a couple of books in Gram's things that belonged to the church. I called Pastor Miles and learned he was staying late, so I brought them over. I'm getting ready to head back to the guest ranch now." She turned back to the older pastor and extended her hand. "Thanks for meeting me, Pastor."

"Of course, Callie. We loved Ada. You're welcome here anytime."

"Thanks. I appreciate that."

As she started to slide past Wyatt, thundering footsteps sounded down the steps.

"Ezra. Andrew. Get back here. Remember what I said about running." A deep voiced echoed in the stairwell.

Two little blond-headed boys raced past them, their laughter bouncing off the walls in the well-lit hallway.

"I said stop!" Troy Branson, the boys' father, rounded the corner. His blond hair was still cut military short. Like Wyatt, he'd left active service to care for his boys. But unlike Wyatt's situation, Troy's ex had abandoned her family, leaving Troy bitter and hurting.

Seeing Wyatt and Callie, he stopped and his shoulders slumped. He held out a hand, but his eyes strayed to Callie. "Hey, Wyatt."

"Hey, Troy. What's going on?" Wyatt clasped his hand and wanted to squeeze it to get the man's focus back on him.

Troy rubbed the back of his neck. "My mom couldn't keep the boys, so I brought them with me, hoping they'd settle down for the meeting. Guess that's not happening. They've been a handful today. I'll load them back up, head home and catch you guys next week."

Wyatt held up a hand. "Hold up. Maybe we can figure something out." He turned to Pastor Miles. "Are you sticking around for a while?"

Pastor Miles clapped Troy on the shoulder. "I'd love to help, but I'm actually on my way to another meeting."

"No worries, Pastor. Thanks, though." Troy jerked his head toward the laughter coming from the room down the hall. "I'll grab the boys and see you next week."

Wyatt stuck out an arm and blocked him. "Stay. Between the group of us, we can manage a couple of boys."

Callie turned to Wyatt. "How long's your meeting?"

"An hour."

She looked at Troy. "I'll watch them while you're at your meeting."

Troy's eyes bounced between Wyatt and Callie. "And you are?"

Wyatt stepped forward. "Callie Morgan, meet Troy Branson. Troy, this is Callie, Ada Morgan's granddaughter."

Trent extended his hand. "That's right. I thought you looked familiar. I was at Ada's funeral. I'm sorry for your loss. She was a nice lady. Made chocolate chip cookies for my boys' birthdays."

"That sounds like Gram."

A crash sounded down the hall. Callie turned to Pastor Miles. "Would it be okay if I kept an eye on them in there?"

Pastor Miles waved his hand toward the room. "By all means. That's the children's room they ran into—the one where they attend Sunday school each week."

"Great, thank you." Callie returned her attention back to Wyatt and Tory and jerked her head toward the noise. "You guys have your meeting, and I'll take care of those little rascals."

"You sure?"

"I can handle two little boys."

"Yeah, I thought so too when my wife left. Boy, they challenge me every day, though. Let me try to get them in line so you don't pull out your hair." Troy headed down the hall.

Callie started to follow, but then Wyatt reached for her elbow. "Thanks for doing this. Troy needs this time, but are you sure we're not keeping you from anything important?"

Callie covered his hand with her own. "This is what's important right now. We'll be fine. If I run into any trouble, you're all just down the hall."

She flashed him a smile that shot him right in the gut.

What was that about?

Standing in the doorway, he watched her walk away. Then he stepped into the adult Sunday school room where the guys were hanging out in groups, clutching cups of coffee.

Wyatt headed for the coffee maker and filled a to-go cup nearly to the top for himself.

A moment later, Troy returned to the room, looking calmer than he did five minutes ago.

He strode over to Wyatt and lowered his voice. "I don't know where you found her, but don't let her go. She got those rowdy boys settled down in less than a minute. If I hadn't given up on women, I'd marry her tomorrow."

Wyatt's gut tightened.

Let her go?

He wasn't bitter toward women like Troy, but

he wasn't in a rush to head to the altar either. His buddy's declaration gave him an uneasy feeling in the pit of his stomach, and he wasn't sure why.

He had no claim to Callie, but he just couldn't make sense of why Troy's words tensed him up.

He needed to shake it off and focus on this week's meeting.

And not on Callie.

Though, if he was being honest, she was beginning to take up more time in his thoughts. And he wasn't sure how he felt about that.

He needed to concentrate on his responsibilities and not the friend from his childhood. He was her boss and her friend. But nothing else.

And he needed to keep it that way.

Chapter Six

If Wyatt said he was fine one more time, Callie was going to flick paint on him.

From the moment she'd seen him at breakfast this morning, he seemed distant. When she tried to review next week's schedule with him, he put her off. Yet, he had time to chill at the picnic table with his brother for half an hour talking about the rodeo.

Whatever.

To be honest, she hadn't expected him to show up and paint as they'd talked about the night before. But he did. And Mia was with him, which made Callie smile.

She pushed her roller in the paint tray, covering it with the lemony yellow color she'd purchased a few days ago from the local hardware store. She applied paint to the wall and moved the roller as high as she could on her tiptoes.

Mia had taken her stool and sat on it while she applied paint with a small paintbrush. She had as much paint on her hands and legs as she did on the wall. At least she'd arrived in old clothes. Or so Wyatt had said when Callie expressed concern about ruining her shirt and shorts.

Wyatt stood on a ladder and applied white paint on the dingy ceiling with an extended roller. He worked silently. Even when he was busy around the guest ranch, he still managed to engage her in conversation. But today? Nada.

Something was definitely going on with him. She didn't know what to make of his mood. And she didn't dare ask what was wrong. No doubt she'd get the same answer—he was fine.

She struggled to keep her attention on the wall. Instead, her eyes drifted toward Wyatt, watching his back as he stretched and moved.

Oh, boy.

She was in trouble.

"Thanks for letting me paint, Callie. I like it." Mia's voice pulled her attention away from the man distracting her from her job.

Callie smiled at the little girl. "You're welcome, sweetheart. I couldn't have asked for a better helper."

"What about Daddy? Is he a good helper?"

"Yes, Daddy's a good helper too."

Wyatt made a noise, and Callie shot him a look. "What was that? Do you have something to add?"

He shook his head. "Nope. Just trying to get things done."

"Do you have somewhere you need to be?"

He didn't say anything. Then he climbed down the ladder and strode over to the paint tray and layered more paint onto his roller. Without a word, he headed back to the ladder.

Callie jumped to her feet and blocked his way. "Hey, what's going on with you? You're quiet today."

"I'm busy."

"You're always busy. That doesn't stop you from having a conversation."

He planted a hand on his hip and glared at her. "Do you want to talk or work?"

Callie gritted her teeth, backed out of his way, then waved her hand toward the ladder. "Work, by all means. Don't let me stop you, Cranky Pants."

"Daddy, did you wear cranky pants today?"

"Callie's silly, sweetheart. I'm fine." Despite the smile he flashed at his daughter, his jaw tightened.

There it was—those two words that set Callie's teeth on edge. She snatched Mia's brush out of her hand and brushed a slash of paint on Wyatt's muscled forearm.

He looked at her with wide eyes. "You put paint on me."

"Yes, I did. What are you going to do about it?"

He looked at her with an expression Callie couldn't decipher. Then he nodded slowly. "I see how it is. Two can play this game." He caught

Callie's arm and encircled her wrist between his thumb and forefinger. Very gently, he removed the paintbrush from her fingers.

Heart already pounding from his closeness, she turned her face as she braced herself for what was to come.

Wyatt grinned for the first time since arriving an hour ago and took a step closer. He waved the paintbrush in front of her. "Let's see how you like it."

She squeezed her eyes shut and tried to pull her hand free. She threw her other hand up to shield him from getting any closer.

Wyatt laughed softly, a sound that rippled through her. Then he captured her other wrist in the same large hand.

Callie could almost smell the paint before the cold, sticky liquid coated her nose. She tried to shield her face, but he kept her hands pinned. She turned her face into her shoulder just as a swash of paint tickled her cheek.

"Wyatt Stone, you don't play fair."

"Oh, I play to win." Wyatt tugged her closer. She opened her eyes and found him smiling down at her. "Give up?"

Part of her wanted to say no so she could still feel his touch on her skin.

Knowing her words wouldn't be coherent, she simply nodded.

"Good. Now hold still." He pulled a red bandanna out of his back pocket, released her hands and reached for the water bottle sitting on the floor by the ladder. After dabbing water onto the cloth, he cupped her chin and gently wiped the paint off her face. "Don't start something you can't finish."

"Daddy, I wanna play too."

"Play? You think we're playing? Mia, my girl, we are doing serious work here." Still holding the brush in one hand, Wyatt scooped Mia up with his free hand and cupped her in his arm. Then he took the paint brush and dotted her nose.

"Daddy!" Her giggles echoed in the empty room.

Wyatt's phone chimed. He set Mia down and pulled it out of his back pocket. He scrolled up the screen. Then he laughed quietly and shook his head. He looked at Callie, smile still in place. "Sorry to leave, but I gotta run. Seems a skunk has decided to take up residence under the deck of one of the yurts. How about if I come back in an hour or so?"

Callie shook her head. "Don't worry about it. I'll clean up here and head back to the guest ranch. I'll come back and paint tomorrow. Thank you for your help."

"Any time."

Callie walked Wyatt and Mia to the door, then closed it behind them.

He may have said 'any time' but she couldn't take advantage of his kindness. She needed to do something to show her appreciation. Maybe bake him some cookies or something.

Hadn't Macey mentioned something about chocolate chip being her brother's favorite?

Callie returned to the shop and poured the paint from the tray back into the gallon can. She should probably take advantage of the time to get more done, but suddenly, she wanted to head back to the guest ranch.

Even though a radio played softly, she missed Mia's giggles and Wyatt's deep voice.

Watching Wyatt playing with Mia filled Callie with longing. In order to have the family she always wanted, she needed to risk her heart.

But it couldn't be with Wyatt. He was completely off limits.

Now she just needed to keep reminding herself of that so she didn't do something silly like falling for her boss and risk losing her job, no matter how much her teenage crush wanted to revive those old feelings.

Wyatt's evening wasn't going as planned. He'd arrived at Ada's cottage ready to paint, just as he'd offered.

But the moment Callie opened the door to the shop, Troy's comment from the other night floated around in his head. And he still didn't know what to make of it. So he'd quietly gone to work. And apparently, that made Callie think he was upset.

How could he tell her what was wrong when he couldn't figure it out himself?

Then, when she slapped paint on his arm... well, he couldn't let that go.

Maybe he'd been out of line to retaliate. All he knew was something was stirring within him that he hadn't felt in a very long time.

His sister Everly's phone call had come at a good time. She'd been preparing the yurts for the incoming guests and complained about the smell.

Since he was the director of the guest ranch, she'd determined he was the best person to take care of the problem.

If it'd happened on any other place on the ranch, he would've ignored the skunk. But he didn't want anything to create a nuisance for their guests. Or risk one of them getting sprayed.

Wyatt knelt on the ground and shined a flashlight under the wooden platform. Sure enough, the beam illuminated a black-and-white hide.

Hopefully, it was a loner. He didn't want a family of skunks living under one of the decks.

Wyatt pushed to his feet and headed for the ranch truck. He retrieved the wire live trap and a peanut butter sandwich he'd made back at his parents' place when he dropped off Mia before heading to the guest ranch.

He carried the trap to the yurt and set it on the ground where the skunk had dug under the lattice. He placed one slice of bread covered in peanut butter inside the trap past the trigger plate.

Since the skunk wouldn't venture out of its new den until dusk, Wyatt pushed to his feet and headed back to the truck. He'd check the trap first thing in the morning.

As he reached for the door handle, metal clinked behind him. He turned and found the skunk inside the trap.

That was fast.

The scent of peanut butter must've been too good to resist.

Wyatt pulled a tarp from the back seat to protect himself from getting sprayed as he hauled the trap to the bed of the truck.

Callie's car barreled down the dusty dirt road toward him. He moved to the middle of the road to stop her.

As she braked, music blared through her open windows. She lowered the volume as he headed to her car.

"Hey, mind waiting here a couple of minutes? The skunk is trapped and I need to get him to the back of the truck without getting sprayed."

"Not at all." She reached for the door handle. "Need any help?"

He raised an eyebrow and shook his head. "And risk you getting sprayed? I don't think so."

"How big is it?"

"About a pound. It's a Western spotted skunk. The ranch has a permit to relocate animals, so I'm moving it to a safer place."

She drummed her fingers on the steering wheel. "I'll stay put until you're done."

With a nod, Wyatt moved away from the car, unfolded the tarp so the skunk couldn't see him. He moved closer to the trap, one quiet step at a time so he didn't spook the skittish creature who'd lifted its tail already.

His booted foot caught on the edge. He stumbled and reached out to steady himself, dropping the plastic material. Wyatt took a step back, crouched and tried to pull the tarp toward himself, but he ended up dropping it again. The rustling sound caught the skunk's attention. It raised its tail again, this time fanning out as the creature stomped its front feet.

Wyatt froze. His heart pounded against his ribs as his chest rose and fell.

The mammal was about to get serious if he didn't cool it.

As he forced his breathing to slow, his phone

rang in his pocket, the ringtone piercing the nearly silent air.

The skunk's head whipped around as it shuffled backward and raised its back end like it was trying to do a handstand.

Before Wyatt could move, the skunk's spray hit him, the putrid odor soaking his side as he turned and tried to use the tarp as a shield.

Having grown up on the ranch and spent a lot of time in barns, Wyatt wasn't a stranger to strong smells, but the skunk spray had him gagging and nearly getting sick in the grass.

He needed to wash off the skunk stench. Now.

Behind him, a door slammed.

Chest tight and his breathing more of a wheeze, Wyatt whirled around and held up a hand. "Callie, don't come any closer."

"Is there anything I can do?" Callie yanked the collar of her shirt over her nose and backed toward her car, but not before a giggle escaped.

Was she laughing?

If this had happened to one of his brothers, he'd be busting a gut. But now that he was the one caught in the line of fire and could barely breathe because of the smell, he didn't find it the least bit funny.

Wyatt pointed to the lodge. "Head inside. I need to call wildlife control and have them remove the critter. Then get this stink off me."

She saluted, then climbed back inside her car and started the engine.

An hour later, he knocked on the door to Callie's suite, his skin still tingling from scrubbing hard to get rid of the smell.

She opened it, then wrinkled her nose and took a slight step back. "Wyatt. Hi."

Apparently, the dish soap and baking soda weren't enough to neutralize the smell.

He stepped away from her door, heat scalding his neck. "You can still smell it, can't you?"

She bit the corner of her lip but it didn't stop a grin from spreading across her face. "There is a lingering scent…"

He groaned. "Great. I'll have to figure out something else to get rid of the odor. I wanted to talk to you for a minute, but maybe I should wait?"

Callie waved toward the water. "Let's sit on the dock. I'll have you sit down wind."

"Laugh it up. At least wildlife control was in the area already and picked up the skunk. Now no one else will get hit like I did."

Leaving the lodge, they walked down the dirt road toward the dock and settled in the Adirondack chairs.

Kicking off her shoes, Callie closed her eyes and lifted her face to the sunshine. The evening rays burnished her hair to a rich gold.

She'd changed out of the jeans she'd worn earlier and into a light blue T-shirt with a sloth curled around a branch, and a white skirt with light blue flowers that brushed against her knees.

He rested his head against the back of the chair and focused on the San Juan Mountains against the cloudless blue sky behind her. "Let's talk, then I'll head back to my place and see what I can do to get rid of the odor."

"We can talk another time, if you'd prefer."

Wyatt laughed. "I've been rejected before, but never because of how I smell."

Callie's cheeks turned a light shade of pink. "I'm not rejecting you. I just don't want you to feel uncomfortable."

"I'll be fine."

"Ugh. That word again."

"Right, the word that brings you to fits of paint rage."

"You just didn't seem like yourself. I wanted to get you out of whatever mood you were in."

"Yeah, about that. It wasn't you. Troy had said something that got under my skin. That's all."

"Okay, I was worried I was adding to your stress by making you paint."

He raised an eyebrow. "Callie, please. I could've said no if I didn't want to be there."

"Like you'd tell anyone no."

"Not anyone I care about." As soon as he

spoke the words, he cringed. What if she got the wrong idea?

Her head jerked up.

Wyatt pushed to his feet before he said anything to embarrass himself. "I need to pick up Mia and get her ready for bed. Then search the internet for a way to take care of this lingering scent, as you called it."

She laughed, shoved her feet back into her sandals, and stood.

They headed up the dock and Callie broke away to the path that led to the lodge. "Have a good night, Wyatt. See you tomorrow."

Wyatt waved and strode toward the ranch truck, feeling a bit lighter than he had earlier.

Talking with Callie had been so easy, just as she had been when they were kids. Which seemed like a lifetime ago now.

If he'd had even a slim desire to date again, Callie was the kind of woman he'd choose for an evening out. But she was his employee now.

And he wasn't about to do something stupid and risk everything by falling for her.

Chapter Seven

Callie simply wanted to show her appreciation to Wyatt for helping with the painting. So, baking his favorite chocolate chip cookies were just a thank-you.

Nothing more. Nothing less.

At least that was what she kept telling herself as she snagged a pot holder off the counter. She opened the oven and pulled out the last tray of chocolate chip cookies. She set the cookie sheet on the stove, then grabbed a spatula and moved them onto the cooling rack.

Scents of melted chocolate, rich butter and brown sugar floated in the air.

Callie ran back upstairs, slid her feet into her new flip-flops, grabbed her purse, then headed back downstairs. In the kitchen, she washed her hands and filled a plastic container with still warm cookies.

Once she cleaned the kitchen, she gathered her things and headed outside.

As she backed onto the road that took her toward the ranch, she nearly braked and turned the car around.

Would Wyatt see the cookies as something more than a thank-you? She didn't want to give him the wrong idea.

She turned down the road that led to his cabin and parked next to his SUV. She pressed a hand against her anxious stomach, then picked up the cookie container before she lost her nerve, and stepped out of her car.

She climbed the steps to the full-length covered porch and knocked on Wyatt's cabin door. She took in the black rocking chair and matching child-size chair sitting near the door. A wooden swing hung at the end of the porch.

The door opened, and Wyatt filled the doorway dressed in a black T-shirt with gold USMC letters across the chest and a pair of gray shorts.

"Callie, this is a surprise."

She thrust the plastic container at him. "Macey said you liked chocolate chip cookies, so I made you some to say thank you for helping with the painting at the shop."

His eyes widened as he took the container and lifted the corner.

"Who is it, Daddy?" The door opened, and Mia peered around his legs. Spying Callie, she pushed through and bounced onto the porch. "Hi, Callie. Wanna come in and see my playroom?"

Before Callie could respond, Mia tugged on her hand and pulled her toward the door.

Wyatt took a step back. "Yes, come in."

"I don't want to intrude."

"You're not intruding, especially when you bring my favorite cookies." He pulled out a cookie and took a bite. Then he closed his eyes and groaned. "Oh, man, these are awesome."

His reaction was exactly what she'd hoped for. "My gram's recipe."

Callie stepped into the open living room with exposed log walls. A rust-colored couch and chair sat in front of a stone fireplace that touched the ceiling. Puzzle pieces lay scattered on a navy-and-rust braided rug. A large flat-screen TV was mounted on the wall above the mantel.

A framed picture of Wyatt wearing his Marine Corps dress blues with his arms wrapped around his wife caught Callie's attention. The top of Linnea's head brushed his shoulders. Her dark hair had been pulled into a pile of curls on top of her head secured by a tiara with a veil trailing down her back. Her strapless white gown with the sweetheart neckline and lacy skirt accentuated her tiny waist. A string of pearls lay against her collarbone.

On the other side of the fireplace, another image in a matching frame showed Wyatt holding Mia as an infant. He smiled in the picture, but the light in his eyes had dimmed.

Even though the photograph was taken only a few years ago, she could see how life events had changed him.

The boyish, almost cocky, glint in his eyes had been chased away by grief. She couldn't even imagine the pain he must have gone through.

She forced her attention away from the man in the pictures to the same one standing next to her. "Very nice."

"Thanks. After I returned to Colorado, we lived at the ranch for a while, then I decided Mia and I needed our own place. This used to be the foreman's cabin. Dad, Bear and I fixed it up for Mia and me to call home."

"You guys did a great job."

Mia tugged on Callie's hand again. "Callie, come and see my playroom."

Callie glanced at Wyatt.

He waved a hand, then bit into another cookie. "Sure, go ahead. I'll be out here eating cookies."

Callie laughed as Mia led her to a small room off the living room. She stood on a stool and turned on the light, revealing walls painted soft pink.

A bright pink child's chair sat in the corner next to a white bookcase overflowing with books. A molded plastic playhouse sat on top of a small square table, the people and furnishings scattered on the floor. Stuffed animals tumbled out of a hammock strung between two windows that cast light across a floral rug that covered most of the wooden floor.

"Mia, what a fun room." Callie knelt on the rug and picked up one of the people for the play-house.

Mia moved to the play kitchen and handed Callie a pink cup. "Would you like some tea?"

"Absolutely. Thank you." She took a pretend drink. "That was the best tea I've had all day."

The little girl beamed. "I'm glad you liked it."

"Sorry to break up this party, but can I talk to Callie for a minute, Mia?" Wyatt stood in the doorway, his hands braced on the frame.

Mia nodded. "You can play in my room any-time you want, Callie."

"Thank you, Mia. I'd like that." Callie pushed to her feet and followed Wyatt out of the play-room.

He stopped in the living room and faced her. "I'm taking Mia into town to spend the night with Ray and Irene. I'll check on the horses, then I'm heading back to the ranch. Would you like to take a ride with me before dinner?"

She tensed, but tried to keep her expression neutral. "Ride?"

He shrugged. "If you feel comfortable enough.

I know they intimidate you, but if you give them a chance, you'll see just how gentle the horses can be."

She thought back to the way Mia engaged with the rescue horses, and Callie found herself nodding. "Actually, that would be a good idea. The more I'm around them, the better that will be for the guest ranch."

"Just the guest ranch?"

Callie shrugged. "After the summer, you won't need me."

Wyatt scowled. "What makes you think I won't need you?"

Her head shot up. "Well…"

"Unless you're planning to look for another place to work, our guest ranch runs year-round."

She raised her eyebrows. "I didn't realize that."

"Didn't I say that when I offered you the job?"

"You may have. To be honest, I was assuming it was a summer gig. I figured you'd shut down at the end of the season."

Wyatt laughed softly. "Even though this summer was the start to our season, we will be accepting reservations through the year, with plenty of activities for every season."

Wyatt turned and touched Callie's chin. "We'd love to have you for as long as you'd like to stay. If you feel the need to look for different employment, I understand. I just ask for a short notice so we aren't left hanging."

"Absolutely. I wouldn't do that to you all."

He jerked his head toward her car. "What do you say we meet back up at the guest ranch in an hour or so and take that ride?"

Callie nodded and fell in step as he walked her to the front door.

On her way back to the lodge, the same question tumbled through her head—was she making a mistake?

The more time she spent with Wyatt, the harder it was going to be to protect herself from any future hurts. Wyatt was her employer, and she needed to remember that.

No matter that her heart longed for more.

After his debacle the other day with the skunk, Wyatt couldn't have made a worse impression with Callie.

Besides, it wasn't like the invitation to go horseback riding was a date or anything. Wyatt wanted Callie to get used to the horses and being in the saddle so she'd be more comfortable around them, especially if she planned to stick around the ranch. What better way than to take her riding?

So why couldn't he stop thinking about her? And what was up with the knot in his gut?

The past few days he'd been hustling Mia out the door so he could get to the guest ranch and see her before their busy days began.

Wyatt parked the ranch truck, then led his black stallion Dante and his mother's mare Patience out of the horse trailer.

He put his sunglasses on, adjusted the brim of his cowboy hat and led the horses to the paddock so they could graze while he waited for Callie.

She walked toward him wearing a light purple button-down shirt with the sleeves rolled to her elbows, faded jeans and cowboy boots. Add a hat, and she'd look like she'd walked off the pages of one of the horse magazines he read online.

He lifted a hand. "Hi, again."

"Hey." She waved back.

Wyatt jerked his head toward the horses. "Ready to ride?"

Something flashed in Callie's eyes. She clasped her hands together in front of her until her knuckles whitened. Then she shrugged. "Ready as I'll ever be, I guess."

"If you're not comfortable, we don't need to do this. I don't want you to be scared."

She shook her head. Her ponytail threaded through her ball cap bounced against her shoulders. "I'm nervous, but let's do this."

He admired her courage.

"Thatta girl. You'll be riding my mom's horse. Patience is as gentle as they come. Plus, we'll go slow. Any time you feel nervous or uncomfortable, we'll stop and walk the horses for a bit. Sound good?" At her nod, he continued. "How much do you remember about getting on the horse?"

Wyatt opened the gate and stepped inside. He gathered Patience's reins and led her to the dirt road.

Callie eyed the mare, then shifted her attention to Wyatt. "It's been so long. Someone held onto the horse the last time I rode. I remember putting my left foot into the stirrup and lifting my right leg over, then settling into the saddle."

"Good memory. I'll hold on to Patience and guide you."

She shot him a wry grin. "Too bad you saddled the horses already. I won't be able to show off my amazing tack skills."

"Next time." He winked at her.

Shaking her head, she grimaced and held up a hand. "No rush. Really."

He laughed. "Like I said, Patience is very gentle. She loves being talked to. Offer your hand so she can sniff you."

She did as he instructed, and Patience touched her nose to Callie's palm.

"She wants you to pet her." Wyatt laid his hand against Patience's neck.

Callie followed his movements and talked softly to the horse.

Wyatt moved in front of Callie and reached for Patience's harness. He lifted the reins over her head and allowed them to rest on her neck. "Hold on to the reins and grab a handful of Patience's mane."

"Won't that hurt?"

"Not as much as pulling on her mouth does. Put your left foot in the stirrup. Lift your other leg over her back and sit carefully in the seat. Try to remain relaxed so she doesn't pick up any anxiety you may have."

Callie did as instructed. The leather creaked as she made herself comfortable. She clasped the reins in both hands.

"Good job." Wyatt reached up and tapped her left hand. "Hold the reins in your left hand. Sit straight but make sure your weight is distributed evenly in the center. Keep your back and arms relaxed, and move with Patience."

Once he felt confident Callie wasn't about to slide off Patience's back or anything, he returned to the paddock for Dante.

His black stallion eyed him, and Wyatt rested a hand against the horse's strong muzzle. "Hey, boy. Let's go for a ride."

He led the horse outside, then slipped his foot

in the stirrup and threw his other leg over the strong animal's back.

Dante nickered, and Wyatt leaned forward and stroked the animal's neck. He gathered the reins and nodded toward the dirt trail in front of them. "Ready?"

Callie nodded, but the look in her eyes had him wondering if her heart matched her head.

He clicked his tongue and nudged Dante with his inner knee. Callie did the same.

He rode down the middle of the trail with Callie to his right along the fence line. She sat straight in the saddle, her arms pinned tightly to her sides, and her jaw clenched. He reached over and touched her arm, her skin smooth and soft against his calloused fingers. "Remember to relax and move with Patience."

As they continued down the path, Callie relaxed a little. While she still sat straight, her arms loosened.

Ahead of them, the late afternoon sun cast a glow across the pasture, spotlighting the rich green grass and turning it to gold.

A light breeze cooled his heated skin and caused purple flowers in the fields to sway. Black and red Angus cows grazed in the fenced pastures. Gray mountain ranges peaked against a cobalt blue sky. The horses' steady clomping set a rhythmic pace and prevented a need to fill the tranquil silence.

Perfect day to forget about his worries.

If only it were that easy.

"Feeling okay?"

She nodded and shot him a tight smile.

The grass stirred beside Patience. A quail flew away suddenly, flapping its wings in front of the mare.

Patience danced back, jerking her head up. Her ears flickered back and forth. Her eyes widened and nostrils flared as she snorted.

Callie shot him a panicked look and pulled on the reins, yanking Patience's head up.

Wyatt brought Dante to a stop, then dismounted quickly. He moved slowly to the mare. Careful to not to get kicked, he reached for one of the reins. He pulled it toward his foot and brought her to a stop. Once she calmed, he pressed a gentle hand on her forehead. "Easy, girl. It's okay. Just a bird."

He glanced at Callie, whose eyes were as wide as Patience's. Her knuckles whitened against the other rein wrapped around her hand. He covered her hands and squeezed gently. "Hey, it's okay. Relax. Breathe. You're safe."

Callie lifted a shaky hand and ran it over her face. "That was…unexpected."

"Yeah. Patience is used to riding the trails, so I'm not sure why the bird spooked her. Are you sure you're okay?"

Callie nodded, but he wasn't convinced. He didn't want her to feel skittish around the horses, especially since she was going to spend much of her summer being exposed to them.

Wyatt lifted his hat and swiped his forearm across his brow as his own heartbeat returned to a steady rhythm.

"Maybe going down the trail was a mistake. Perhaps we should've ridden around the arena at the ranch until you're more familiar with being in the saddle again."

She shook her head. "No, I'm good. I promise. Let's keep riding."

"You sure?"

She expelled a deep breath, then rolled her shoulders. Gathering the reins in her left hand again, she nodded.

Wyatt mounted Dante, then turned the horse until he faced her. "The horse rescue is up ahead. I can feed and water the horses quickly. Or we can return to the guest ranch."

"I'll give you a hand."

He shot her a smile. "We'll make it a quick trip, I promise."

As they rode toward the back gate, Callie's arms and shoulders relaxed.

"You appear less tense on Patience, considering the way she spooked a few minutes ago."

She laughed. "I'm a great pretender. She is a

gentle horse, but that was a little scary for a moment. Hopefully nothing else distracts her again."

"Yeah, that was a little weird for her to react that way, but we handled it."

"We? More like you. I tried not to panic."

"Not panicking is a huge part of it."

The trail widened, and he dropped back alongside Callie rather than walking in front of her. "The back gate is around this next bend. We'll ride through the pasture and head to the barn."

Ahead of them, the trail forked. The right path led them to his in-laws' horse farm.

A couple of chestnut Morgan geldings grazed along the fence line. They lifted their heads. Seeing Wyatt and Callie, they bolted across the pasture.

Callie sucked in a breath.

"You okay?" Wyatt turned to her.

She pointed toward the skittish horses galloping away from them. "I'll never get used to seeing their ribs."

Wyatt's jaw tightened as he nodded. "Ray rescued them from a kill lot a couple of months ago. They were malnourished and abused. They won't let him near them, but they are coming into the barn now, so that's a plus. Another reason why what Ray's doing is so important— protecting these beautiful animals and giving them peace."

"I really admire what you guys're doing."

"Thanks. We can't do it alone, but it can begin with just one."

Wyatt led the way into the barn, then dismounted. He held on to Patience while Callie practically jumped off her back. He hid a grin as she winced and put her hands on her thighs.

She was going to be sore tomorrow.

Wyatt showed her where the grain was kept and how to add it to each feeder attached to the stalls. While she did that, he headed upstairs and dropped bales of hay through the floor door. When he returned to the first floor, she'd filled the final feeder.

He pulled apart one of the bales and dropped flakes of hay in each of the stalls. Then Wyatt showed her how to rinse the buckets and refill them with fresh water.

Charlie, the blind pony, nickered as Callie approached his stall. Callie talked to him in a soothing voice as she had earlier to Patience. The horse's ears perked as he lifted his nose and nuzzled her palm.

"You're much calmer than the last time you visited Charlie. That's what he needs."

She turned to him, her eyes filled with sadness. "I can't stop thinking about the visible ribs on those other two horses."

"It gets me too." He waved a hand across

the stalls. "The good news is that all ten of the horses Ray's brought to the rescue are beginning to thrive. We're done with feeding, so let's head back to the guest ranch. Dinner will be served soon, then we'll have a campfire. Planning to stick around?"

She nodded, but kept her eyes on the pony. Then she fell in step with him as they headed to the door. "I just don't get it."

"Get what?"

"How people can mistreat animals like that."

"I hear you. If I can help make a difference with at least one, then that's one horse who will have a new purpose."

"Is there anything else that can be done?"

Wyatt laughed low in his throat. "There's always plenty that needs to be done. Problem is, Ray's stubborn and won't let me do much. I did manage to talk him into offering monthly sponsorships. So now the sponsors come on a weekly basis to care for their horses and help with the grooming, but there's always something that needs to be done."

"I'm sure every bit helps." He held on to Patience while Callie mounted her, with a little more confidence this time. "What about you? Your time is maxed out too."

Wyatt's fingers curled around the saddle horn. "I'm fine."

"Right." Her raised eyebrow showed she didn't believe a word he said.

He settled himself in the seat and guided Dante through the pasture. "I still hope I can talk Ray into agreeing to turning this place into a sanctuary."

"What's holding him back?" Callie moved alongside him.

"Asking for help was tough for Ray, and I don't think he's ready to relinquish control just yet. I'd love to be a partner and keep him invested without having to carry the burden."

"You'd carry it for him. That's what you do."

Wyatt lifted a shoulder. "I'm fine."

"There's that word again. When was the last time you weren't fine?"

Wyatt squinted against the sun and swallowed several times as a memory of Linnea's funeral surfaced—one he rarely allowed himself to see. "The night my wife died."

Callie leaned over and laid a hand on his shoulder. "Of course. I'm sorry. I shouldn't have been so callous."

He drew up the reins and brought Dante to a stop. He looked at her, then focused on the field next to him. "When I was a kid, my mom and I were in an accident. She hit her head pretty hard and needed to be taken to the hospital by ambulance. I was terrified and maybe even crying, I think. She tried to reach for me and comfort me, but one of the police officers pulled me back. He was a gruff old-timer who knew my grandparents. He said I needed to be strong and brave and hold it together for my mom's sake. She was upset enough and couldn't worry about me too. At the hospital, everyone praised how brave I was being. So ever since, that's what I do—I keep it together for everyone else so they don't worry about me."

"Oh, Wyatt. That cop was so wrong. It's not up to you to carry everyone else's emotions."

He dismounted and reached for Patience's harness. "After Linnea died, I left the Marine Corps instead of re-upping and came back to the ranch because I wasn't strong enough for my daughter. I kind of fell apart, and it wasn't fair to her."

Callie climbed down and faced him. Her eyes shimmered as she pressed a hand against his cheek. "You'd lost your wife. Your response was expected and even necessary. How many times have I said grief is tricky? Just when you think you're fine, those waves of emotion crash over you, threatening to drown you. You're strong, but not because of your muscles or how you hold it together for everyone else." Her hand moved slowly to his chest and she palmed the area around his heart. "You're strong because of your faith that feeds your strength and empowers you to keep going. You don't have to be fine around me. Be you, no matter how you feel."

Wyatt sucked in a breath as her words swirled around in his head. Other than family, no one had worried about him since Linnea. He missed having that special someone in his corner.

What would it be like to have someone to lean on again? Someone to see him and still support him when he was feeling weak? Someone to hold his hand without telling him to suck it up?

Someone like Callie.

Without taking time to think it through, he covered Callie's hand, then slid his fingers into hers. He drew her closer and cradled her other cheek.

Her breath caught and her eyes widened.

He lowered his head and kissed her gently. She released his hand and slid her arms around his neck as he tightened his embrace, breathing in the scents of sunshine, fresh air and the barn.

A moment later, he reluctantly dragged his mouth away from hers and released his hold but didn't let her go. She pressed her cheek on his chest and he rested his chin on top of her head, trying to get a handle on his ragged breathing.

Until this moment, he'd kissed only one woman in his life, but she was gone.

What would it be like to put the past where it belonged and focus on his present...and perhaps his future?

Falling in love meant risking his heart once again. He wasn't ready to do that. Or was he? What about Callie? She had her own pain to work through.

Would she want to take the risk too?

Chapter Eight

Callie wasn't speechless very often, but that unexpected kiss had stolen her breath…and her words.

She wanted nothing more than to stay in Wyatt's arms forever, but they needed to get back to the guest ranch.

She closed her eyes as she listened to the steady rhythm of his heart in her ear. She needed to say something, but she was afraid to lose this moment.

What had he been thinking kissing her like that? And what did that mean moving forward? Did she dare ask him? What if she didn't like his answer?

"You're quiet."

"I'm not sure what to say."

"I hope I didn't upset you."

Her head jerked up, nearly connecting with his chin. "Upset me? How?"

"By kissing you."

She shook her head, a little more forcefully than necessary. "No. Not at all."

"So you wouldn't be upset if I did it again?"

"You want to kiss me again?"

A slow smile spread across his face as his hands slid down her arms.

She soaked in the feel of his embrace, a place she'd dreamed of for years as a teenager.

But they weren't kids anymore, and this couldn't be a summer fling. At least not to her.

Wyatt tipped up her chin. "What are you thinking, Callie?"

"That I've wanted to do that since I was fourteen."

He laughed softly and drew her against him once again.

"But I also want to be sure this is happening for the right reasons," she said.

"What would those right reasons be?"

Ignoring the voices in her head screaming not to, she stepped back from him. She gazed at Dante and Patience grazing close by. Wrapping her arms around her waist so she wouldn't reach for him again, she looked at him. "The day I came to Stone River was supposed to have been my wedding day."

His eyes widened. "Are you serious? You never said anything."

She shrugged. "I didn't want to talk about

it. Instead of walking down the aisle on what should've been one of the happiest days of my life, I holed up at an unfamiliar guest ranch, cried myself to sleep, then woke and decided to figure out what was next for my life."

"What happened? With the wedding, I mean. Although, if you don't want to share, that's fine. I get it."

She shook her head. "It's okay. Shawn and I had a difference of opinions."

"Every couple has differing opinions."

"True, but I believed I should have been the only woman in his life. He believed that he could cheat on me with a coworker and everything would still be okay."

"What a jerk."

"I could have forgiven him and worked it out through counseling, but then I learned she was pregnant. With the three of us teaching at the same elementary school outside of Denver, it would've been so awkward." Callie glanced at her bare hand where the carat diamond used to be. "I taught art while he taught Phys Ed and coached high school track. My parents were in Chile, and my brothers were in college. When Gram had her stroke after Christmas, I decided to take a leave of absence to care for her. I'd call Shawn nearly every day to stay connected, but he'd talk only a few minutes, claiming to be busy. He gave me some excuse as to why he couldn't come to Gram's funeral. I decided to head back to Denver without letting him know so I could surprise him. When I went to his apartment, he wasn't home, but his girlfriend was. And it was apparent she'd been there for a while. I went to the track at the high school where he was coaching, gave him back the ring, and told him to have a nice life."

"Wow, Callie, I'm so sorry. That stinks."

Tears clouded her vision as the humiliation surfaced all over again. "Gram tried to tell me Shawn wasn't the right guy for me, but I wouldn't listen."

"Love is blind for a reason."

"I don't know. I mean, I'm not even sure if I truly loved him. I think I loved the idea of being with him and starting a family someday. Once my parents left for South America, I was so lonely and he filled that void." She blew out a breath and faced him. "So, I guess those right reasons would be you kissed me because you wanted to kiss *me*. Not because you're lonely or the circumstances felt right."

Wyatt laughed softly as his mouth slid into another slow half grin. He reached for her hand and drew her closer. He traced his thumb over the curve of her cheek. "Until today, I've kissed only one woman in my life. And she's gone. I can't change that. What I can change is my future. Since I saw you on the side of the road that day, I haven't been able to stop thinking about you. I kissed you because I wanted to. I find myself thinking about you even when I'm busy with very little time for anything else."

Standing on her tiptoes, Callie brushed a light kiss on his lips. "Thank you."

"For what?"

"For being honest."

Wyatt pressed his forehead against hers. "Honesty creates some complications."

"Such as?"

"Well, technically, I'm your boss."

Callie's stomach tightened as her gaze dropped to the toes of her boots. "I'd forgotten about that. Does this mean I need to quit? Find a teaching job?"

"Only if that's what you want. Personally, I love being around you."

"It may not be that simple."

"Why not?"

"While I love working at the ranch, teaching offers benefits such as insurance and retirement."

"Again—is that what you truly want to do?"

"No, but I may need to settle. Especially if Gram's shop proves to be more work than it's worth."

He tipped her head until he captured her eyes with his and framed her face with his hands. "Callie, listen to me. Never settle. Not with me or anyone else. Not with doing what you love. God gave you a talent, and He will show you the way it's to be used."

She mulled on his words. Being with him wouldn't be settling. Definitely not. But she couldn't say that. Not now. And maybe not ever.

For the first time in three and a half years, Wyatt didn't want to be sitting in the basement of his church, surrounded by the dozen or so single fathers who'd become like brothers to him.

He'd started the single father support group when Mia was only six months old, and the weekly get-togethers had helped him through the trials and challenges of single parenting.

Sure, he'd had his family helping out, and he'd truly appreciated them. After losing his wife and trying to be both mother and father to his daughter, he'd needed to be with guys who understood. Guys who walked the same road. Guys who could rally around one another and help them get through life.

Tonight, he realized he'd rather be back at the guest ranch, seeing Callie as she managed the daily activities, played with the kids, picked flowers with his daughter and smiled at him.

At least she was only a few doors down caring for Troy's two boys. When she learned Troy's mom couldn't watch the boys any longer, she'd offered to care for them so he could attend the support group.

One more reason why he couldn't stop thinking about her. In fact, it took everything in his power to remain in the room.

He looked around at the guys who sat on beige armchairs and half a dozen folding chairs in a semicircle, holding ceramic mugs of strong coffee and eating blueberry muffins he'd picked up from his aunt's diner.

Wyatt headed to the coffee maker and topped off his cup. Then he took one of the empty armchairs near the front of the room. He placed his mug on the side table, leaned forward with his elbows resting on his knees, and clasped his hands. "Okay, guys. How about if we get started? Who wants to lead the prayer?"

Troy raised his hand. Once the rest of the guys found places to sit, he opened in prayer.

Amens echoed around the circle.

Scanning the room, Wyatt rubbed his hands together. "How's it going?"

Several of the guys bobbed their heads, but no one spoke immediately.

Ryan, one of the newer members of the group, set his cup on the floor, and then braced his forehead in his hand. "Well, I went on my first date since my marriage ended two years ago. Paid through the nose for a sitter. Got dressed up. Met her at a nice restaurant in Durango."

Wyatt raised an eyebrow. "How'd that go?"

Ryan shook his head. "Disaster, man. Absolute disaster. This whole online dating thing is not for me, I guess. She didn't like the food. She talked about reality TV shows. I think I only said three words the entire night. We definitely weren't a match." He imitated holding a phone and swiping. "I'd like to meet a nice girl at church. Not some phony who shows up looking nothing like her profile pic."

A couple of the guys burst out laughing and nodded. "Yep, been there, dude."

"At least you tried, man." Troy, sitting in the chair next to Wyatt, lifted his chin toward Ryan. Then he glanced at Wyatt. "When should we start dating again? My wife left two years ago as well."

Wyatt rubbed his hands on his thighs, then reached for his coffee. "I don't have that answer, man. It's different for everyone. You feeling ready?"

He shrugged. "I don't know. Who has the time? After working all day, I have to pick up the boys from day care, feed them, bathe them, spend time with them, and then it's bedtime. Plus, there's dishes, laundry. How do you find the time to even look for someone to date?"

"I hear you. I'm right there with you. You guys all know what it's like to manage a busy schedule."

Troy jerked a thumb toward the back of the church where children's laughter could be heard. "At least you have it easy."

Wyatt scowled. "Easy? How do you figure that?"

He grinned. "Callie. Your new guest ranch manager."

Wyatt's stomach tightened as he straightened in his chair and seared Troy with a direct look. "Yeah. What about her?"

"Just sayin', man. You're spending all that time together. You trying to say nothing's going on between you two?"

Wyatt clenched his teeth as he tamped down on the words choking his throat. Needing to get a grip, he leaned back in the chair and tried to look relaxed. "Callie and I are just friends. I've known her since we were kids. I told you that."

"Just friends, huh?"

"That's what I said."

Troy's eyes narrowed as he shot Wyatt a wolfish grin. "So, you'd be okay with me asking her out?"

Wyatt fisted his fingers. "I wouldn't suggest it."

"Why not?"

"Because then I'd have to deck you, and I don't want to mess with the group dynamic like that."

Troy let out a howl and slapped his leg. He thrust a finger at Wyatt. "I knew it, man. I've seen the way you watched her. What's going on?"

"I told you—we're just friends."

"Aww, come on, Wyatt." Troy circled a finger around the group. "We're tight, right? What's said here stays here."

Wyatt scanned the group of men who'd experienced similar types of loss and dragged a hand over his face. He stood, moved to the door and closed it, shutting out the laughter from down the hall. His hand tightened on the knob. "Callie and I are just friends."

"You keep saying that." Troy leaned forward. "But…"

Wyatt held out a hand. "A gentleman doesn't kiss and tell."

As soon as he'd said the words, he wished he'd kept his mouth shut. Especially when whoops, hoots and claps erupted around the room. Heat climbed up his neck.

What a bunch of jerks.

Troy shot him another grin, looking very pleased with himself. "You kissed her."

It wasn't a question but a statement.

One that Wyatt couldn't refute. And he didn't want to. He'd thoroughly enjoyed that kiss. And hopefully, he could do it again.

But he wasn't about to share those intimate details with a bunch of guys. Or with anyone else, for that matter. That was private between him and Callie.

But he could share what was in his heart, especially if it gave the other guys the hope they needed to move forward in finding a second chance. Wasn't that why they were there—to support each other in all areas of their life?

Wyatt settled back in the chair and took a sip of coffee. "I've known Callie for years. Growing up, she used to visit Ada during summers and holidays, and we'd hang out. She recently moved to Aspen Ridge and needed a job, so I offered her one. I had no intentions of getting involved with her or anyone else. While I'll always love my wife, I'm beginning to realize I do not have to live the rest of my life alone. I'm not in a rush to get married, but let's just say I'm a little more open than I was even a month ago."

He palmed his cup with his left hand, and his ring clicked against the ceramic. He looked down at the platinum wedding band. He set the mug on the table. Taking a deep breath, he wiggled the ring, very slowly, from side to side and slid it off his finger.

Releasing his breath, he held up the band that he had worn for nearly a decade. "Linnea and I married so young. Never in a million years did I expect to lose her giving birth to our daughter. Celebrating Mia meant remembering what we'd lost that day over and over and over again. The other night, Callie and I went riding. And we talked. The kiss wasn't planned, but it happened, and I don't regret it."

He paused, swallowed past the lump in his throat and tightened his fingers around the wedding band. He glanced at his left hand, where only a pale line remained. "I'm ready to move on. But, to be honest, I really have no idea how to do it."

He reached for his coffee cup again and his fingers trembled slightly. Instead of forcing the band back onto his finger, he stretched out a leg and slid the ring into his front pocket. Then he wrapped both hands around his cold cup before he could yank it back out of his pocket.

A slow clap sounded, then escalated.

Wyatt's head jerked up. Troy stood and placed a hand on his shoulder. "That took guts, man."

Wyatt glanced at him. "The kiss?"

Troy shook his head. "No, bro. The ring. You really are ready to move on."

He stared into his mug. "Thanks, man."

He pushed to his feet and walked to the coffee

maker to refill his cup. Taking a sip, he turned back to see the guys still watching him. "I think many of us are ready to move on. Maybe the best way to do it is to take that first step. Meet the girl. It's not going to be easy. I've watched Macey and Bear muddle through their relationships. But now they have their families. And I want that, too."

Troy planted a fist on his hip. "I can't speak for anyone else, but fear is a great motivator to stay single. My wife was the girl next door. Or so I thought. I didn't realize she was living a secret life as an alcoholic. How could I have been so blind? Now, part of me is afraid to take a chance because how can I trust my own instincts when I screwed up so badly the first time?"

Murmurs rumbled through the room as heads nodded. Several of the guys had gone through a divorce. A couple, like Wyatt, were widowers. And a couple had become single fathers out of wedlock.

"I don't know what to tell you, Troy. You can't paint everyone with the same brush. And I think that goes for the women we meet and decide to date." Wyatt removed one of the Bibles off the bookshelf behind him and held it up. "We need to stay true to God's Word. Give your fears and frustrations over to Him. Ask for His wisdom and guidance as we step into the dating pool once again. He'll connect us with the right women. When He's leading the way, and we're walking in step with Him, then we won't go wrong. We'll find those relationships that will, hopefully, last a lifetime."

Before anyone could comment, a cry sounded from down the hall. A moment later, someone knocked on the door.

Troy crossed behind Wyatt's chair and opened it. Callie stood in the doorway, holding one of his sons in her arms. Three-year-old Ezra had a red mark on his cheek and tears running down his face. "I'm sorry for interrupting, but Ez fell off his chair and smacked his cheek on a toy. He wants his daddy."

Troy took his son from Callie and gathered him in his arms. "Hey, buddy. What's going on?"

"I fell. I hurt my cheek."

Troy kissed his son's cheek, then used the hem of his T-shirt to dry the little boy's face.

"I'm sorry that hurt. Daddy's in a meeting. Will you be okay with Miss Callie for a couple more minutes?"

He nodded and wiggled out of Troy's arms.

Wyatt's eyes connected with Callie's. She mouthed, "Sorry."

Wyatt shook his head and waved away her apology.

She lifted the little boy in her arms, pressed

a kiss on his red cheek, then guided his head to her shoulder. She gave the group a wave. "Sorry, guys."

Troy closed the door and pressed his hand against the frame. Then he turned and locked eyes with Wyatt, his face serious. "Wyatt, I'm going to give it to you straight, man. Let go of your fear, and take a chance on that woman. Because if you don't, someone else is going to snatch her up very quickly. She's the kind of girl that we're all looking for."

Wyatt nodded, digesting his friend's words.

Troy was right.

Callie was the kind of woman he could see being a part of his life.

Even though he was now a little more open to the idea of having a relationship, was he ready for a real date?

He couldn't answer that. He needed to take his own advice—ask God for wisdom because he didn't have much faith in his own.

Chapter Nine

Callie couldn't be more pleased with the way the shop was shaping up.

And that was partly thanks to Wyatt and his willingness to help.

Even though the walls were now refreshed with a lemony yellow paint that made the main room seem so much bigger and brighter, Callie couldn't keep ignoring the upstairs if she wanted to stay on schedule with the new reopening.

Fatigue settled in her bones, and her muscles ached from moving different pieces of furniture back in place. She decided against refinishing the floors, choosing to scrub them by hand and oil them to bring out the shine.

Now she wanted nothing more than to turn off the cottage lights and head back to the guest ranch and get some sleep.

No campfire for her tonight. She needed to carry the boxes upstairs to be sorted later. Then she could collapse into bed.

Only to do most of it all over again tomorrow.

Cradling a box of stained glass supplies against her stomach, Callie headed for the back steps. Her foot paused. And she sighed.

This was ridiculous. She needed to go up sooner or later. She couldn't avoid it forever.

Closing her eyes, she exhaled, then opened them and forced herself to climb the dimly lit staircase.

She turned the knob that led to Gram's apartment for the first time since the funeral, pushed it open and nearly tumbled back down the steps at the rank, musty smell.

She dropped the box on the floor beside the small table inside the door and winced at the sound of breaking glass.

Callie hurried through the small four-room apartment, trying to find the source of the odor.

The smell worsened the closer she came to the bedroom with the attached master bath. Forcing her attention away from Gram's neatly made bed, Callie pivoted toward the bathroom door and opened it.

The stench had her stumbling away from the doorway.

She pulled the neck of her T-shirt up over her nose as she fought to gain control of her gag reflex.

Black mold spotted the lavender rug in front of the sink. Brownish water stains rippled across the dated linoleum. The bottom edge of the vanity doors bulged.

Breathing through her mouth, Callie flung open the door and groaned.

Greenish-brown rust corroded the drainpipe under the sink, causing a hole where water trickled down the side.

Callie checked the plastic knobs, but they were off.

So where was the water coming from? Why couldn't she smell it downstairs?

After the funeral, she'd convinced her parents to keep the utilities turned on because she expected to spend a lot more time at the shop than she had.

Callie grabbed the corner of the throw rug and held it at arm's length. She carried it into the small kitchen and tossed it into the bagless trash can. She'd deal with that later.

She returned to the bathroom and grabbed a handful of towels out of the narrow linen closet next to the shower. She knelt in front of the vanity, folded several and piled them around the leaking pipe. They were soaked with water within seconds.

What was she going to do? Maybe her dad would know.

She grabbed the top of the vanity with her wet hand and started to stand. Her fingers slipped. As she tried to catch her balance, her foot slid out from under her on the wet floor. She slammed her right arm and shoulder against the tub and dropped her weight on her wrist.

A pop sounded and fire shot up her arm. She grabbed her arm and cradled it against her body as she tried to stand again. Again, her foot failed to gain traction.

Tears filled her eyes as the pain rippled across every nerve. Her head pounded as her stomach churned. Using her left hand, she pushed away from the vanity and scooted across the floor until she reached the doorway. She stretched, grabbed onto the doorknob and pulled herself into a standing position.

Bile clawed at her throat as her head swirled. She blinked several times and stumbled to her grandmother's bed.

With shaking fingers, she pulled out her phone and then paused.

Who could she call?

The lights were off next door, so she knew that Ray and Irene weren't home.

Exhaling, she called up Wyatt's number on her phone and pressed the speakerphone button.

After three rings, he answered, "Hey, Callie."

"Wyatt, I need you."

"What's wrong?"

"I'm at the shop." Her heart raced as tears blurred her vision. "There's a water leak. And

I fell. I can't move my arm or shoulder. I don't know what to do." Her voice cracked. She dropped her head in her hand and pressed her thumb and middle finger against her soggy eyes.

"It's okay, Callie. I'm coming. I'll be there in fifteen minutes. Okay?"

"Okay."

He ended the call.

Pushing off the bed, she clutched the phone and made her way through the apartment and down the stairs. She found her purse on the counter next to the register and lifted it over her head and across her body.

Then she sat on the wooden bench and waited.

She clutched her upper arm and sucked in a sharp breath as another realization hit.

Without her teaching job, she no longer had medical insurance. And very little money left in her savings. How was she going to afford a trip to the ER?

Moving to Aspen Ridge had drained her. In more ways than one.

If she had a broken arm or wrist, how was the injury going to affect her job? And the work that needed to be done at Gram's shop?

What if she needed surgery like Ray?

Her heart raced as the what-ifs seared her brain. Sweat broke out on her forehead as the heaviness tightened in her chest.

The back door flew open. "Callie?"

"In here." Her voice came out as a squeak.

Wyatt strode through the shop and knelt in front of her.

The sight of him sent a wave of relief through her and she burst into tears.

He pulled her against his chest and gently wrapped his arms around. "Hey, it's going to be okay. I'm here."

As much as she wanted to believe him, he couldn't be more wrong.

Despite his assurances, it wasn't going to be okay, and Callie had no idea how she was going manage to open the shop now.

After returning from the emergency department with an emotionally wrung-out Callie, Wyatt had tossed and turned most of the night.

The heaviness in his chest beat away any hopes of sleep.

Somehow, though, he'd managed to drift in the early hours. And he must've hit snooze or turned the alarm off altogether because he woke up to a cute little girl sitting in his bed with Ella the Elephant and her favorite book.

She giggled when he threw back the covers that landed on her head and hurried out of bed. But he wasn't in a playful kind of mood.

He had a team to lead.

But first, he needed coffee if he was going to function today.

"Wyatt, you in there?" His mother's voice sounded muffled as she knocked on his front door.

Wearing only his jeans and T-shirt, he hurried out of the kitchen and to the living room in his bare feet. His big toe hit the edge of the door as he opened it. He groaned loudly in pain.

He yanked the door open. "Hey, Mom."

"You okay? You missed breakfast. And your dad said you didn't show up for chores this morning."

Wyatt dragged the edge of the towel over his face. "Yeah, sorry about that. I overslept."

Mom crossed her arms over her chest and shot him a pointed look. "You never oversleep."

"Yeah, well, I did today." He cringed at the growl in his voice.

Stepping inside, she shot him the same mom look he'd gotten many times as a teen when he'd gotten mouthy. "I was afraid of this—you're overdoing it. What's going on?"

The way her voice softened and held compassion took him back to the years when he could crawl into her lap and she'd make everything better.

He forced a smile. "Nothing, Mom. I'm fine."

She folded her arms over her chest. "When

you were younger, you got in trouble for lying to me."

"What are you going to do? Ground me?"

"Oh, honey, if only it were that simple." Mom's forehead creased as she pressed a hand against his unshaven cheek. "I worry about you."

Wyatt brushed a kiss across her knuckles. "No need. I'm good. I'll grab some socks and boots and meet you at the guest ranch."

"If Mia's ready to go, I'll take her back to the ranch with me to save you some time."

"Thanks, Mom." He kissed her cheek, hoping to smooth out the lines creasing her forehead. "I'm fine—I promise."

Fifteen minutes later, with a steaming to-go mug of coffee in hand, Wyatt stepped out of his SUV. He headed across the grass where three families gathered around picnic tables enjoying the buffet his mom and Everly had made.

Morning sunshine streamed through the trees, striping the ground in gray and gold. A breeze blew through the leaves. A boy around five or six chased after a wayward napkin.

Callie sat in the shade by the lodge along with two girls who had to be around nine or ten. She'd laid her right arm—which was in a wrist splint—on the picnic table. Colored pieces of glass lay on a tray between them. Sunlight glinted off the shards, sending a spectrum of colors across the table.

As he moved closer, his shadow stretched across the table. "Morning."

Callie looked up and shielded her eyes. "Good morning."

"Sorry for being late. I overslept. How's it going?"

"Good. We're making faux stained glass suncatchers. Want to join us?"

"Suncatchers? Like what your grandma used to make? Is that safe?"

"These are faux suncatchers. We're using acetate and Sharpie markers to color in our designs. They're outlined with black glue to mimic the soldering. Perfectly safe."

He looked at the girls who were using permanent markers to color in their designs. One had made a heart while the other had created a rainbow.

He shook his head. "No, thanks. I have to get the horses ready for the trail ride."

"Bear and your dad left already."

"What do you mean they left already?"

"The trail ride started half an hour ago. When you weren't here, Bear called your dad. They both took the guests for this morning's ride."

"I wish you'd called me."

Callie's lips thinned. "Check your phone."

Setting his mug on the end of the table, Wyatt dug out his phone. Three missed calls. And a text from Callie—Hey, sleepyhead, get out of bed. There's work to do.

He'd never heard the phone ring. In his haste to get out the door, he hadn't bothered checking his messages either.

"Well, that's just perfect."

"Sit with us and relax a minute. It's okay to take a break."

"I said I don't have time." His words came out so sharply that both girls' heads shot up. They looked at each other with widened eyes, then ducked down to focus on their designs. Callie's cheeks turned as bright as the hot pink marker in her left hand.

He dragged a hand over his face. "I'm sorry."

She nodded but kept her attention on the piece of half-colored plastic in front of her.

He touched her shoulder. "Hey, you got a minute?"

She looked up and he jerked his head to the open doors that led into the lodge.

Her lips thinned again, but she nodded. "Sure." She looked at the girls. "I'll be right back."

They nodded as their eyes darted between Callie and Wyatt.

Great first impression, idiot.

Wyatt followed Callie into the lodge where the

scents of coffee and bacon lingered. His stomach grumbled, reminding him of his lack of breakfast.

That wasn't all he lacked.

Moving so she could still see outside, Callie cradled her right arm against her chest, raised an eyebrow and waited.

Yeah, he deserved that.

"Look—I'm sorry for snapping at you. I didn't mean it. I've been kicking myself for oversleeping and worrying my mom. I'm sorry for taking my frustration out on you." He touched her splint. "How's your wrist?"

"Painful. Sleeping last night wasn't fun. I'm trying not to do much. Which is tough, since I'm right-handed."

"Anything I can do to help?"

She raised an eyebrow. "You don't have time, remember?"

"I deserved that." He rubbed a hand over his jaw.

"Why is it okay for you to worry about others but no one's allowed to worry about you? You're taking care of everyone else, but who's taking care of you?"

"I'm fine."

"Right. And that's why you overslept. Your body is protesting your lack of sleep. Wyatt, I'm worried about you."

He held up a hand. "Don't. You have no reason to."

"That's right. You're fine. My mistake." She dropped her arms to her side, then winced. Cradling her right arm against her stomach, she pushed past him.

He reached for her elbow. "Callie, wait."

She stopped but didn't turn.

He dropped his hand and blew out a breath. "I'm sorry. I know you're just being a good friend. I'm just not used to people worrying about me."

She whirled around, her eyes full of fire. "Then you're blind. If you'd take half a second to look around you, then you'd see how much your family worries. I've seen how your parents watch you. Everyone wants to be sure you're okay."

"That's just it—they have enough to worry about without adding me to their problems. I'm fine."

"If I had a dollar for every time you said you were fine, I wouldn't need to worry about money to renovate Gram's shop."

His jaw tightened. "I just don't want anyone to worry about me."

"Stop saying that! Why not?"

"Because it leads to heartbreak." The unexpected words felt like they'd been yanked from his chest, leaving a gaping hole exposing all of his vulnerabilities.

Needing some air, he tightened his grip on his nearly empty coffee mug and strode through the doorway. As he headed for his SUV, he kicked himself about a thousand times.

Hiring Callie was a mistake.

Not because she couldn't do the job, but because she was a distraction.

Problem was, he couldn't exactly let her go.

Somehow, he needed to figure out a way of working with her without letting his guard down.

Even though he'd said he was more open to letting someone in his life, actually doing it was a different matter.

Maybe he was kidding himself. Maybe he wasn't ready after all.

Chapter Ten

Why did Callie allow Wyatt's mood to get under her skin, especially since she was the reason for his late night?

If she hadn't called for help after getting hurt, then he could've been home and gotten the sleep he needed. Spending five hours in the emergency room wasn't fun for anyone, but he'd insisted on staying even after she said she could drive back to the guest ranch.

She just needed to put him out of her mind and focus on the rest of her day. After all, the guy was entitled to an off day, just like anyone else.

Problem was, he wasn't just anyone else.

At least to her.

And that really bugged her because she couldn't be falling for someone so soon after her breakup. Didn't matter that she'd known Wyatt for years. A month ago, she'd been about to get married.

She needed to get a hold of herself and focus on doing her job.

Now that the guest ranch families were either

kayaking with Bear and Piper or hiking with Deacon and Nora, Callie needed to figure out a plan for the mess at the shop.

During breakfast, she'd asked Deacon and Nora for recommendations for plumbers and she called the first name they'd given her. Thankfully, the guy on the phone offered to meet with her that afternoon once she explained the situation, including her injured wrist.

She pulled into the empty space behind Gram's shop and parked next to the Pullman's Plumbing truck. Stepping out into the sunshine, she shielded her eyes as a tall man waited for her on Gram's back porch.

Wayne Pullman.

The man who was going to give her good news or ruin the rest of her day.

Removing his stained ball cap and revealing dark hair streaked with silver, he nodded to her. "Hey, there, Ms. Morgan."

"Mr. Pullman. Call me Callie. Please." Cradling her right arm, she stuck out her left hand.

He took it, giving her a firm shake. "Callie. Sorry to hear about your wrist."

"Thanks. I can deal with a fracture. I'm glad it wasn't worse."

If she had to guess, she'd say he was in his fifties. Or at least closer to her parents' ages rather than hers. Deep lines grooved his tanned face.

He nodded toward the door. "Let's head inside and see what the problem is."

She unlocked the door and stepped into the same room she'd visited several times over the past few weeks. Gram's faint scent still lingered despite the windows Callie had opened to air out the rooms.

Wayne gestured toward the second floor. "You said it was the upstairs bathroom, right?"

Nodding, Callie led the way up to the empty apartment.

Forcing herself to keep focus on the problem at hand and not the memories begging for her attention, she showed Wayne the way to the small bathroom and flicked on the light.

The door to the vanity hung open, revealing the same corroded pipes and base spotted with mold. She stepped back and gave him room to inspect the damage.

Wayne lay on the floor, pulled a small flashlight out of his shirt pocket and shined it against the underside of the sink basin. He made a few comments to himself, then slid out from under it and pushed to his feet.

"Yeah, as I expected, the seal around the water valve gave out." Wayne did a little bounce in front of the vanity. "Feel that spongy floor?"

She followed his movements, then nodded. "What about it?"

"Because the leak wasn't caught for a while, stagnant water soaked into the floor. A drip or two may not seem like a big deal, but when it goes unnoticed, it can create a lot of damage."

"I kind of expected that when the mat in front of the sink was wet and covered in mold. Pretty gross."

He crouched in front of the vanity and pulled up a lifted corner of one of the linoleum blocks. "With this much damage, the subflooring and joists may need to be replaced. Maybe even the walls, depending on how much the water damage has spread."

Callie's shoulders sagged as she leaned against the doorframe. "What about the shower and toilet?"

"Because of their age, I'd recommend replacing them as well so you don't have problems in the future, but it also depends again on the damage to the floor."

She glanced at the heavy porcelain tub and matching toilet that had been in Gram's apartment for as long as she could remember. "Hopefully it's minimal. I'd like to hold off replacing them until I take care of higher priorities."

Wayne headed out the door and waved her to follow. "Let's head downstairs and see if there's damage to the ceiling in the room below."

Again, she followed, her stomach tightening with every step.

Wayne disappeared into the small studio located behind the stairs where Gram held her classes. Hands on his hips, he stood in the middle of the room and looked up at the giant brown stain on the popcorn ceiling. "The ceiling needs to be replaced. But until we tear it out, we won't know the extent of the damage. We'll have to replace the insulation and all that. I'm concerned about the wiring as well. This house is pretty old, so I suspect it could be knob and tube."

"So, you're saying there may be an electrical issue in addition to plumbing repairs?"

"Honestly, we won't know until you get a qualified electrician to check it out. But if I were to speculate, then, yeah. Sorry. I know that's the news you don't want to hear." Wayne pulled a pen and small notepad out of his back pocket. He made several notes, then tore off the sheet and handed it to her. "I've been in this business for over thirty years. I won't have an exact cost until I can get back to the office, but here is a ballpark figure of what I'm estimating for repairs. In the meantime, I'll shut off the main water valve so the leaking stops."

Callie took the paper and scanned the scrawled numbers while Wayne shut off the valve. As she reached the total, her stomach clenched and she sucked in a breath. The estimate was way more than she had expected.

How was she going to afford this?

They talked for another minute, then turned off the lights and headed back outside. Callie locked the door.

She remained on the back porch while Wayne got into his truck and drove away.

Needing to get back to the ranch, she climbed into her car. She pressed a thumb and forefinger to her tired eyes. "Sorry, Gram, I don't know if I can afford to keep my promise."

As she backed down the drive, she remembered the Help Wanted sign in the animal shelter window she'd seen when she arrived in town.

Maybe Irene still needed help?

Could she manage another job while working at the guest ranch and trying to find time to get Gram's place ready?

She braked and headed for the front door to see if the sign was still in the window.

It was gone.

Maybe Wyatt's aunt Lynetta needed help at the diner. She wasn't sure when she'd have time, but she'd find it to earn the money needed for the water damage. Besides, it didn't hurt to ask.

Callie parked in front of the yellow-sided corner restaurant. Purple and yellow pansies spilled out of the window boxes attached to the front wall. White rockers sat on the newly added covered porch that spanned the front of the building.

She headed inside, the bell on the door signaling her arrival, and breathed in the rich scents of coffee, french fries and baked goods.

"Hi, Callie."

Callie turned in the direction of her name and found Mia standing in the booth next to her dad, waving her arm.

Callie moved toward their table. "Hey, Miss Mia. How're you doing?"

"Good. I went to the dentist. He counted my teeth." She gave Callie a toothy grin, then held out a limp fry covered in ketchup. "Want a french fry?"

"Thanks." Callie took it, careful not to drip ketchup on her gray T-shirt.

"Hey, Callie. Have a seat." Wyatt gestured to the empty space across from him.

She raised an eyebrow. "You sure?"

"Yeah, sure. Sit. Tired of ranch food?"

"No, actually, I stopped to see if Lynetta needed help at the diner." She set the soggy fry on the napkin Wyatt pushed toward her.

He eyed her a moment, then leaned back against the booth. He slung one arm over the top of the vinyl seat, then reached for his coffee. "You quitting on me? Because of this morning?"

"Nothing like that." She pulled the notebook

paper from the plumber out of her purse and slid it across the table to Wyatt. "I need money to pay for renovations. The water damage I discovered last night at Gram's house comes with a hefty price tag. Managing the guest ranch is great. But it's not enough to pay for repairs, much less renovations. Even if I drain the rest of my savings." She held up her splinted wrist. "Especially when those medical bills come rolling in."

Wyatt scanned the numbers, then he whistled quietly. "Man, I hope Wayne's not pulling a fast one on you."

"Is it too high?"

"Not for a guy who runs his own business, but it may break your budget."

"I don't have a budget. Just a pipe dream. I want to make good on my promise, but the shop may be nothing more than a money pit." She didn't expect the sudden rush of tears and blinked rapidly to keep it together.

She was so tired.

"Don't rush into a decision based on frustration and emotions. A couple of the guys in my support group may be able to tackle this project at half the cost. Let me make some calls and get back to you."

She slumped against the back of the booth. "That would be great, Wyatt. Thank you. I appreciate it."

"Don't sweat it. They're a good bunch of guys who don't mind helping out."

"Even for someone they don't know?"

"They know me, and they knew Ada. And they've seen what you've done to help Troy. That's enough." He winked, causing her heart to skid against her ribs.

Once again, Wyatt had come to her rescue. Somehow, she needed to repay him without losing her heart in the process.

Wyatt was right—Callie shouldn't settle. Not in her relationships. Or with her desire to live her life the way she wanted. And she planned to share that information with her father who was bound to ask about her future plans.

Callie had exactly seven minutes to find the courage to let her parents know she hadn't applied for local teaching jobs like they'd been hoping.

The microwave beeped, and Callie removed her mug. She unwrapped a chai tea bag and dropped it into the hot water. Then she set the mug on the table next to the love seat and reached for her laptop.

She crossed her legs and winced. Even a week after her ride with Wyatt, she still couldn't move without her body aching. Who knew it took so many muscles to ride a horse?

But she needed to get used to it if she planned to stick around.

After that kiss, she wasn't in a hurry to leave. The guest ranch or even Aspen Ridge. Ever.

Her phone chimed, signaling an incoming video call. Instead of answering, she opened up her laptop and clicked on the join call button.

Three other boxes popped up as her brothers and parents appeared on the screen.

She smiled and waved. "Hey, guys. How's it going?"

Both brothers had dark hair and green eyes like their parents, but Wesley looked more like their dad while Trevor favored their mother's side of the family. Both boys towered over her and used her head as an armrest every chance they had. Which wasn't too often these days.

Dad's thinning hair had more gray than the last time she'd seen him several months ago. Both of her parents had a look of peace that shone in their eyes.

Callie reached for her tea and settled into a more comfortable position as her brothers took turns talking about their summer jobs at the hospital near their campus. Then her parents gave an update on what was happening with their newly planted church.

Wesley, her youngest brother, folded his arms

and leaned back in his gaming chair. "You've been quiet, sis. What's going on with you?"

Callie shrugged, then winced. She rubbed the muscle in her upper arm. "Keeping busy at the guest ranch and working on the shop in my spare time, which isn't a whole lot."

Dad leaned forward and tilted their computer so they showed up better on the video. "Shouldn't you be applying for teaching positions?"

And there it was.

Callie's fingers tightened on her mug. "I'm not going back to the classroom, Dad."

"Callista, are you sure that's the best choice?"

Her father was the only person who used her full first name, especially when he was annoyed and didn't want to show it.

"It's the best choice for me. At least, right now. I gave Grandma my word. I'd think you'd want to see her legacy continued."

Mom laid a hand on Dad's arm. "Honey, she struggled to keep that shop afloat. We don't want you to have to struggle like that."

"Part of Grandma's struggle was not understanding technology. She did things the old-fashioned way. Once I reopen, I'll have a website set up along with social media accounts for advertising. I'll manage inventory and billing on my laptop."

"What about the building itself?"

"It needs some work." Not wanting a lecture, she didn't share the recent water issue with them.

Dad rubbed his jaw, then drummed his fingers on the table, shaking the laptop. "All right, then. If you're serious about this, we can help. Mom left us a little money too."

She shook her head. "No way. She left that for your church plant."

Someone knocked on her door.

"Hang on a minute. I'll be right back." She set her laptop on the cushion and hurried to the door.

She opened it and found Wyatt leaning against the doorframe. Her heart picked up speed. "Hey, Wyatt. What's up?"

He gave her a long, lazy look as a slow smile spread across his face. "I missed you. Busy?"

She ran a hand over her hair, cleared her throat and waved a hand toward the love seat. "I'm, uh, on a video call with my family."

He pushed away from the doorway, straightened, then took a step back. "Sorry for interrupting. I won't keep you. I'm heading to the rescue in a bit to tend to the horses if you want to give me a hand."

Alone time with Wyatt? Yes, please.

She glanced over her shoulder once again, then back at him and nodded. "I'd love to help. I'll give you a call when I'm done talking with my family."

"Sounds good." He winked as he walked backward toward the steps.

How was she supposed to return to her family after that?

She closed the door and then returned to her computer. "Sorry about that."

Mom raised an eyebrow. "Was that Wyatt Stone?"

"Yes, I'm going to go help him feed and turn out horses in a bit."

"He's cute. And single."

"Don't, Mom. I don't need someone else managing my love life. Falling in love only leads to heartbreak."

Dad wrapped an arm around Mom's shoulders and pulled her close. "Not always, honey. Give yourself time and you'll find the right man. Just make sure he treats you right."

Shawn had said all the right things in the beginning of their relationship, and look how that turned out.

But Wyatt was nothing like Shawn.

She shook her head. "I'm not sure Wyatt's ready to move on yet. He still loves his late wife. I won't compete with someone else again. Learned my lesson with Shawn."

"Shawn was unfaithful. Wyatt is a widower. There's a big difference."

"I don't have time to fall in love if I'm going to get Gram's shop reopened."

Trevor scooted closer to his computer. "Hey, sis. I'm sure you don't want to hear this, but I'd rather you heard it from us."

Callie had a feeling she knew what her brother was going to say, but she needed to hear it anyway. "Spill it."

"Shawn got married."

Just as she expected.

"When?"

"Last weekend."

"Last weekend?! A month after we were supposed to walk down the aisle? That's beautiful. Well, I wish him all the happiness in the world."

"Do you?" Wesley raised an eyebrow.

"What do you think, Wes?"

"I think he's a jerk, and you deserved better."

"Thanks, buddy."

After another couple of minutes, they said their goodbyes and ended the call.

Callie closed her laptop and pushed it onto the other cushion, then buried her face in her left hand.

A burst of laughter echoed from outside.

Callie glanced at her watch. Probably too late to call Wyatt now. He would've left for the rescue by now since he hoped to be back in time for the campfire.

She slipped her shoes on and headed for the door. Maybe a s'more would lighten the heaviness in her chest.

She hurried down the steps and headed out to the fire ring near the lake.

Wyatt's family and several of the guests had gathered in chairs around the crackling fire. Smoke spiraled toward the sky.

"Callie."

The sound of Wyatt's voice spiked her pulse as her heart slammed against her ribs.

She turned as Wyatt walked up to her. "You didn't call, so I figured you changed your mind."

"Actually, I just hung up with my family. Did you go to the rescue yet?"

He shook his head. "Want to join me?"

"Yes, but I meant to bring down a sweatshirt. I'll run back upstairs, grab one and meet you down here."

"Mind if I walk up with you?" That same slow smile from earlier that turned her stomach to jelly creased his face.

"I don't mind. But won't your family miss you at the campfire?"

He glanced over his shoulder, and then looked back at her. "They're fine. They won't even know I'm gone." He frowned and tipped her chin. "You okay?"

She clasped her hands and dropped her gaze to her feet. "I'm fine."

"Who's the fibber now?"

"So you do admit you're not always fine."

"This isn't about me. You okay?"

She lifted her hands, then dropped them at her sides. "Yes. No. Maybe."

"Glad you clarified that. I love a woman who knows her mind."

Did he just say *love*?

Don't be ridiculous.

It was a joke. Nothing more.

"So, what's going on?"

The sincerity in his voice brought her head up and she locked her eyes with his.

"My ex got married last weekend. Can you believe that?" She scoffed and yanked on the door with a little more force than necessary.

Wyatt palmed the door over her head and held it for her to pass through. "And that upsets you."

"I don't know how I feel. I'm certainly not in love with him anymore. He's a jerk. I just… I don't know. We dated for four years before he even proposed. And then, it wasn't even a solid proposal. More like a suggestion. But with her, it was a matter of months." Callie's flip-flops slapped against the steps as she stomped up the stairs.

"So, if you're not upset, then…" His voice trailed off.

Callie whirled around so quickly she nearly slipped off the step. Wyatt caught her and steadied her. "I was thinking what you said during our ride."

"What's that?"

"That I shouldn't settle. With him I would've settled. I'm glad we're no longer together. I just wish…" She sighed and shoved her fingers through her hair.

She didn't even know what she wished for.

She turned and ran up the rest of the stairs.

At her door, Wyatt took a step toward her and reached for her hands. "Maybe you're wishing for what could've been. Or maybe what should've been. Your breakup with him does not mean you have to spend the rest of your life alone."

Again, the warmth in his tone nearly undid her. She blinked back unexpected tears. "That means learning to trust and risk my heart all over again. What if another guy breaks it?"

Wyatt's eyes darkened as he ran his knuckles over her cheek. "Then he'd be an idiot."

She reached for his hand and squeezed. "Thanks. I don't know, maybe it's time I moved on too."

"What do you mean by moving on? You mean like with this job? With your life?"

"Not the job. I love it here. It's exactly what I needed when I arrived back in town. So thank you for that."

He tipped his hat at her. "Why, certainly, ma'am."

She laughed at his terrible Western drawl.

She opened the door to her suite and flipped on the light.

At least she'd made her bed today and tidied up before she left for breakfast.

Wyatt leaned against the doorframe while she grabbed a hoodie out of the closet.

She pulled it over her head and gathered her hair back into a quick ponytail.

"Okay, I'm ready."

But he wasn't looking at her.

In fact, he was looking at something over her shoulder.

She turned and groaned.

The watercolor she'd been working on lay on the small table.

He took a step toward the table. "May I?"

She wanted to grab it and toss it under the bed. Instead she shrugged and stiffened, waiting for some generic comment.

Wyatt lifted the paper and studied the watercolor she'd begun the morning after arriving at the guest ranch. His brows furrowed as his lips thinned.

He hated it.

"Callie." His voice came out as a whisper.

She fought back a shiver as she braced herself and lifted her chin.

But she didn't see disgust in his eyes. Instead, she saw something like…wonder, maybe?

The lines disappeared on his forehead and around his mouth as he shook his head and waved a hand over the pad. "This is incredible."

Her cheeks warmed as she dropped her eyes to her toes. "Thank you."

He took two steps toward her and tipped her chin up to meet his eyes, his face serious. "I mean it. This is really, really good. There was a flyer hanging at the diner advertising an art show in Durango. You should submit this."

"What? No way." She reached for the painting. "It's not good enough. I think I told you already—it's the first time I'd picked up a brush since Gram died. It's far from my best work."

He let out a laugh. "If that's not good enough, then I can only imagine what your best looks like."

She glanced at the landscape depicting the ranch complete with a black horse like Dante, added after their ride, drinking from the river running through the property. "You really like it?"

"No."

She knew it.

He laughed. "No, I love it. I love the way that you captured Stone River and the ranch. And Dante."

She picked up an archival ink pen and scrawled her name and date in the corner. She held it out to him. "You can have it."

His eyes widened as he reached for the painting. "Are you serious?"

She hated how vulnerable she felt at the moment. "Sure, but don't be showing it around. It's not that great."

"You are severely underestimating your talent. Anyone who looks at this could see that." Still holding onto the paper, he cupped her cheek and ran a thumb over her jawline. Then he kissed her. "I've been waiting to do that for a week."

Callie's hands tightened on his arms. "What was stopping you?"

"I didn't want to rush you. You're going through a difficult time right now and I didn't want to take advantage of that."

"I appreciate that, but my feelings for my ex died the moment his girlfriend opened the door. His betrayal and the humiliation over my stupidity hurt more than losing him."

"Maybe it's time we both took a chance."

"What are you suggesting?"

The downstairs door slammed open. "Wyatt,

you in here? Ray called—you're not answering your phone. Wants to know if you're planning to feed the horses."

Hearing his brother's voice, Wyatt sighed and touched his forehead to hers. "Can we pause this conversation for the time being?"

Callie nodded, not quite sure her voice was strong enough to answer anyway.

Just what *was* Wyatt suggesting?

She didn't want to jump to conclusions and end up humiliated again, but if he was thinking what she was hoping, then she was all in.

Because being with Wyatt certainly wasn't settling.

And she'd simply have to trust that he wouldn't break her heart.

Chapter Eleven

Wyatt refused to let Ray's gruffness get to him. If the man needed someone to blast, better it be him than Irene.

He could take it. And ignore it.

He'd arrived at the rescue to feed and turn out the horses and found Ray sitting in the barn. He mentioned something about getting into an argument with Irene about his physical therapy sessions and needing some air.

Ray leaned on the walker he had graduated to using over the crutches. "I'm worried about her."

Wyatt didn't need to ask who. "She's a strong woman, Ray."

"Even strong women have their breaking points, Wyatt. I don't want my health to take a toll on her."

"Yes, they do, sir." Wyatt dug the pitchfork into the hay and removed soiled bedding. He dumped it into the wheelbarrow, then poked the fork into the hay. "Go apologize for being...well, your grumpy and stubborn self. She'll forgive you. She always does. Then focus on healing instead of fighting her about doing your therapy exercises."

Ray closed his eyes and rubbed his forehead.

Wyatt returned to mucking the stall, tossing clean bedding against the wall.

"I want you to have the rescue."

Wyatt's head shot up. "Excuse me?"

Ray opened his eyes and sighed. "You heard me."

Wyatt's fingers tightened around the handle of the pitchfork. "You want me to have the rescue?"

Ray shifted and sat on the walker seat. He braced his elbows on the handles and clasped his hands in front of him. "Irene and I talked last night, and we're in agreement—we want you to have the rescue and turn it into the sanctuary Linnea always wanted."

"But—"

Ray scowled and jabbed a finger in Wyatt's direction. "Son, you've been pestering me for weeks now to buy the horse rescue. Now that I'm giving it to you, you're arguing with me? Make up your mind."

Wyatt exited the stall and leaned the fork against the wall. He moved in front of Ray and held up a hand. "I'm not arguing. I guess I'm not understanding why now."

Ray lifted his hands and then dropped him back in his lap. "What's not to understand?"

Wyatt blew out a breath and forced a patient tone into his voice. "Why do you want to give me the rescue?"

"I just told you…to turn it into the sanctuary that Linnea always wanted."

"I get that. But why now?"

"I'm not able to get around like I used to. Time to face facts."

"Come on, Ray. Don't talk like that. Once your cast is off, you'll regain strength in your leg and be back at it in no time."

"I'm not being a pessimist, but a realist. Take the rescue and begin the proceedings to turn it into a sanctuary so you can qualify for those grants you talked about. That way Mia will have a legacy of her mama. But there are a couple of conditions."

"Such as?"

"Irene and I will keep the house and the animal shelter, but you can use the barn and the ranch as you see fit. I promise not to question or argue."

"I don't know what to say."

"Thank you will suffice."

"Thank you."

Ray reached over and gripped Wyatt's wrist. "You're the son I never had. After Linnea was born, we learned Irene couldn't have more children. She cried because she couldn't give me the son she thought I wanted. But I was more than thrilled with my baby girl. Unfortunately, I didn't have her long enough to let her know how much she meant to me." The older man's voice cracked.

Wyatt rested a hand on the man's shoulder. "She knew. She loved you guys with everything that she had."

Ray swallowed several times and nodded. He closed his eyes, but not before tears drifted down his cheek. "Irene and I have been talking about you."

Wyatt could handle Ray's grumpiness and brush it off. But this...this display of raw emotion that was so seldom seen...well, that was a little harder to come to grips with.

Wyatt worked his jaw. "That's what I've been hearing."

"You could've turned your back on us after Linnea passed, but you stuck around. Made sure we have plenty of time with Mia. You will always be our son. Mia is our granddaughter, of course. Just want you to know your future wife and any other children you have will be family too."

"I appreciate that, sir, but I just don't know if that's going to happen anytime soon. I could buy the rescue as a partner. You don't have to give it to me."

"Nope, it's a gift. If you ask to buy it one more time, then the deal's off and I'll sell it to someone else."

Once all the stalls had been cleaned, Wyatt returned to Stone River. Instead of turning down the dirt road that led to his cabin, he headed for the guest ranch.

His head swirled with his conversation with his father-in-law. Callie was the first person he wanted to share the news with.

He parked and looked around the guest ranch, but no one appeared to be in sight. He headed into the lodge, climbed the steps to her room and knocked on the door.

She opened it, a towel around her shoulders as she dried her damp hair. "Wyatt. This is a surprise."

"Disappointed?"

She shook her head as a slow smile sent his pulse racing. "Not at all. I just came back from kayaking with the Pollens. Bear and Piper took the Lairds fly-fishing down the river while the Herricks took their granddaughters into town for ice cream. What's up?"

He pressed his hands against the doorframe and blew out a breath. "Mind if we go for a walk?"

The light dimmed in Callie's eyes, but she nodded. "Sure. Just give me a minute to finish drying my hair. How about I meet you downstairs?"

"Sounds good." He pushed away from her door and headed down the steps.

His sister Everly came out of the kitchen carrying a tray of graham crackers, marshmallows, peanut butter cups and chocolate bars.

"Hey, Wy. When did you get back? How's Ray?"

"Just now. Ray's doing okay so far. Thanks for watching Mia for me." He glanced around the room. "Where is she, by the way?"

"Mom had to run into town, so Mia went with her. They'll be back in a bit. You sticking around for s'mores tonight?"

"Sounds good."

Wyatt turned and sucked in a breath. Callie had changed into a pair of jeans and a red, short-sleeved, button-down shirt. But it was the cowboy hat that nearly did him in.

"Look at you, city girl. Fitting in with the locals."

She posed and gave him a saucy look. "When in Rome, right?"

"I don't know about Rome, but you definitely fit in at the ranch." Wyatt took her hand and held it up as she twirled.

"You look great, Callie. Love the hat."

Callie's eyes widened as if she realized, for the first time, that they weren't alone. "Thanks, Ev. I found it at my grandma's."

"I'll see you guys later." She shot Wyatt a pointed look.

Wyatt placed a hand on Callie's lower back

and ushered her outside. "Let's walk the trail where we rode a couple of weeks ago, if you don't mind?"

"The one that leads to your in-laws' rescue?"

"Yes, and that's what I wanted to talk to you about anyway."

"Okay." Uncertainty filled her voice. "Is something wrong?"

"Just the opposite, actually."

As they walked, Wyatt slid his hand into Callie's and told her about his conversation with Ray. He tried—and failed—to keep his excitement contained. All the way back to the ranch, his mind had buzzed with ideas for improvements.

"That's nice." She smiled tightly. Callie released his hand and slid her fingers in her front pockets. "I'm happy for you."

Wyatt gave her a puzzled look. He bumped his shoulder against hers. "Nice? That's all you have to say?"

She stopped and faced him. Even though her sunglasses shaded her eyes, she wouldn't meet his gaze. "Yes, it's nice. I'm very happy for you. This is what you've wanted for a long time."

"Callie." He touched her arm. "What's going on?"

Hands still in her pockets, Callie straightened her arms and shook her head. "Nothing."

He really hated when people said nothing and there was definitely something.

"You sure?"

She shot him a bright smile. "Yes, I'm positive. I'm very happy for you, Wyatt. This is something you wanted to do for a long time and it relieves a lot of stress for Ray and Irene. They wouldn't give it to you if they didn't think you could handle it. They really love you and trust you."

While the words sounded sincere, Callie's eyes had lost their spark.

Had he done something to cause the change?

Callie would never call Wyatt a liar, but was he really being truthful with himself?

He'd mentioned he was ready to move forward, but his excitement over the horse rescue made her wonder if he truly believed it.

She *was* happy for him. And for Mia. She deserved to have a reminder of her mother.

While walking with Wyatt, she'd given him a noncommittal answer when he asked if she was going to the campfire.

Technically, she was on her own time. So, instead of going to the lake, she chickened out, snuck out the back door and headed into town.

Callie exhaled and brushed the back of her

hand across her forehead. She should've been up-front with him instead of being a coward.

The men in Wyatt's support group had fixed the plumbing under the upstairs bathroom sink, replaced the damaged floor and ceiling on the first floor. She couldn't thank them enough, especially when they refused payment for their labor. Thankfully, the materials didn't wipe out the rest of her savings like she'd expected from Wayne's estimate.

She needed to finish painting the trim work and the windows, then she'd feel a real sense of accomplishment.

She grabbed the can of white paint off the counter and set it on the drop cloth on the floor. As she reached for the metal opener, someone knocked on the back door.

Wyatt.

She wiped her fingers on a towel, then headed to the door and opened it.

Instead of Wyatt, Jacie Brewster, her new friend from church who owned a bridal shop in town, stood on the back porch. She wore a cropped denim jacket over a cute sundress covered in yellow sunflowers. Her blond hair was piled on top of her head and her makeup was perfect. Next to her, Callie felt like a grungy mess.

Callie opened the door wider. "Jacie, come in. I'm surprised to see you."

Jacie waved a hand toward the animal shelter. "I needed to drop something off to Irene for our women's ministry event coming up and saw your lights on, so I figured I'd stop by and say hi."

She reached out to give Callie a hug, but Callie put her hands up before the woman could get too close. "I'm a mess."

Jacie hugged her anyway. "You're never a mess, Callie."

"I'd offer you something to drink but I'm not really living here at the moment."

Jacie smiled. "No worries. I can't stay long anyway. Aaron and I are going out for dinner, but I wanted to talk to you about something. I know we just met at church, and you don't know me well. I adored your grandma, and I miss her very much."

"Me too."

"She used to brag on you all the time. She shared the watercolor cards you sent her. Anyway, I wanted to let you know my brother just bought an art gallery. He's looking for an art director, and I told him about you. He asked me to give you his number if you're interested. You should call and talk to him about it. The job offers good pay and solid benefits. I know you mentioned wanting to get your grandmother's shop reopened so you don't have to return to the classroom, but give this some thought."

Jacie pulled a card out of her pocket and held it out to Callie.

She took it and ran her thumb over the embossed logo. "Where's his gallery?"

Jacie scrunched up her face. "Well, that's the thing… It's in the Springs."

"Colorado Springs? That's like five or six hours from here, isn't it?"

"Yeah, something like that."

She tapped the card against her palm. "Thank you. I'll think about it."

"I hope you don't think I'm out of line by telling you about it."

"No, not at all. I'm flattered you'd think of me, but there's a lot to consider. For one, I'm not sure I'm qualified." She waved her hand around the shop. "Plus I promised Gram I'd reopen the shop, and I hate to go back on my word."

"I totally understand. Brian—that's my brother—is willing to talk if that's what you decide. Even if it's only to learn more about the position." Jacie looked at her smartwatch. "Hey, I have to run. Let's get together soon, okay?"

"Sounds good." Callie walked her to the door.

After Jacie left, the desire to finish painting waned, but Callie needed to make the most of the little time she did have. She dipped her roller into the paint and applied it to the wall.

The art director position was so tempting. She

did have her degree in art history, but she had no gallery management experience. Would helping at the guest ranch count? Probably not.

Not everyone offered jobs as easily as Wyatt.

The idea of decent money and benefits was appealing, but were they enough to move again?

She loved Aspen Ridge. If she did leave, she'd have to start all over again. Not to mention she'd have to sell the shop and forgo her promise to her grandmother.

She needed to consider Wyatt and Mia too… and whatever it was she had with them.

Callie just didn't know what to do. Her mom would tell her to pray about it.

But what if she didn't like God's answer?

Chapter Twelve

Bear was getting on Wyatt's last nerve.

"Did you hear me?" Bear raised his ax and split the pine log in half.

"I heard you. Trying to decide if I want to answer you or not."

"It's a simple question. What's going on between you and Callie?"

Had Bear asked yesterday, Wyatt would've had a different response. But right now, he had no idea.

Shrugging, he grabbed the wood and piled them on the stack for the next campfire. Turning his back to Bear, he stared at the lake. "We're friends."

"Right. Friends. Nothing more? Why don't I believe you?"

"That's on you, man."

The late afternoon heat sent a trail of sweat running down his back. He wiped his face with the hem of his T-shirt and reached for his water bottle.

"I see how you look at her. You haven't shown interest like that in any woman since Linnea."

Having been awake since 4 a.m., Wyatt was feeling the effects of his very long day. And his patience was about shot.

He arched his back, then straightened and glared at his brother. "Like I said, I don't know what's going on with Callie and me, okay? I thought things were good. Then I told her about Ray giving me the horse rescue and… I don't know. Her attitude changed. She congratulated me, but her body language didn't match her words. Then she skipped out on last night's campfire. I feel like she's been avoiding me."

"What do you think that's all about?"

"I don't know, man. Your guess is as good as mine. Being married was so much easier than the single life."

"Amen, brother." Bear held out a gloved fist, and Wyatt bumped it. Then his brother waggled his eyebrows. "But then, I do have the best wife."

Wyatt laughed. "I think Dad might disagree with you. And Cole. And probably every other decent man on the planet. A good husband thinks his wife is the best."

"You're probably right. At least any man who is strong enough to treat his wife with the respect she deserves." Bear pulled off his gloves and drained the rest of his water. He wiped his mouth with the back of his hand, scattering wood shavings stuck to his skin. "How's the search coming for an assistant trail guide?"

"I've been too busy to look. I took Callie riding. Once she's more used to being in the saddle, I'll see if she can help out when you're busy. You have a lot going with getting the rehabilitation ranch up and running. Not to mention needing time with Piper and Avery."

"Brother, I am always here for you. You know that." Bear grabbed him around the neck.

Wyatt clapped his brother on the back. "I do, and I appreciate it. I plan to ask Callie about staying on as manager after the summer season ends."

"What about her shop?"

Wyatt shrugged. "Only she can answer that. I just know I like having her around."

Bear grinned. "I knew it."

"Yeah, well, don't get cocky. And keep it to yourself."

"No worries. Speaking of Callie…" Bear jerked his head toward the guest ranch. "Doesn't look like she's avoiding you any longer."

Wyatt glanced over his shoulder and found Callie walking toward them.

Pulling off his gloves, Wyatt turned around. He couldn't stop the smile at seeing her even if he wanted to…which he didn't. "Hey, Callie. What's going on?"

She jerked a thumb over her shoulder. "Things are quiet at the guest ranch. Everly and your mom are helping the kids make cookies in the lodge while the Yaegles went on a hike. I'm going to head into town for a bit and do some more painting at the shop."

Wyatt checked the time. "I need to pick up Mia from Ray and Irene's. Mind if I go in with you?"

Callie shook her head. "Do you want to take one vehicle or drive separately? I'm only going to be gone a couple of hours. Then I'll be back for tonight's evening trail ride."

"You're planning to ride with us?" He tried to keep the eagerness out of his voice.

"If there's enough room. Families have first option, of course, but I'd love to go back out and give Patience another chance."

"I'm glad her getting spooked didn't scare you away for good. Since I have to pick up Mia, and she needs her booster seat, how about if I drive?"

"As long as you have me back in time. My boss is a stickler."

Happy to see the Callie he'd come to know, Wyatt bumped her shoulder. "Don't worry about your boss. I know how to handle him."

"Give me a minute to grab my bag."

He nodded toward his SUV parked next to her car. "I'll meet you there."

"Sounds good."

After she walked away, Wyatt turned back to his brother. "Sorry, man. I'm ditching you."

Bear held out his hands, palms up, and lifted them as if they were scales. "Chopping wood with your brother or hanging out with the pretty girl." He tossed a balled glove at him. "Pretty girl wins. Get out of here."

Wyatt grabbed his work gloves and slapped them against his thigh. He fished out his keys and headed to his SUV.

Callie met him at the passenger side, and he opened her door. "After you."

"Thank you."

Wyatt started the engine and headed toward Aspen Ridge. At the red light, he stopped and turned to Callie. "Hey, I have something to ask you."

"What's up?"

"Are things okay between us?"

"What do you mean?"

The light turned green and Wyatt headed through the intersection. "Your tone and body language changed after I told you about the horse rescue."

"I was being an idiot. I'm sorry, Wyatt. That was me. Not you. I guess I'm still trying to process some things."

"Like what?"

"My ex marrying so soon after our breakup kind of threw me. I know you wanted this horse rescue for a while. And it's always been your dream to turn it into a sanctuary in your wife's memory. And I think that's beautiful."

"But?" He glanced at Callie.

"Don't forget about me being the idiot part." She ran a thumb over her fingernails. "I just wonder if there's room…"

"Room for what?"

"For me." She exhaled as if she had been holding her breath.

Wyatt pulled the SUV over to the side of the road and shifted into Park. Then he turned, resting his left arm over the steering wheel, and reached for Callie's hand. "I'm not going to lie, Callie. I loved Linnea very much, and I always will. We had a solid marriage. We were so excited about expecting Mia and growing our family. When she died, that dream died with her. Her death nearly broke me." He released her hand and pressed his against his chest. "She will always hold a place in my heart. But I believe there's room for more."

Then he lifted his left hand that still felt a little naked. "Notice anything?"

Callie lifted her face, her eyes tangling with his. Her cheeks reddened. "You are so brave. I'm sorry for sounding so jealous. Especially over someone who isn't even here."

"Jealous, huh? That must mean that you like me."

Callie blinked a couple of times, then looked out her passenger-side window. Then she faced him again and squeezed his hand. "Wyatt, I've liked you for a very long time. And I think you want to like me, but…man, could I sound any more like a fourth grader?"

Again, he couldn't stop the smile that spread across his face. "I'm so glad to hear that." He traced the line of her jaw with his hand. "You are so beautiful, Callie. You are sweet and kind and Ada would be so proud. My family and I had a conversation about you the other night."

"Me? Good, I hope."

"The best. We're all in agreement. We really admire everything you've done at the guest ranch, especially since this hasn't been an easy time for you. You've really made your mark. Some of our success is due to your friendly attitude and the way that you took control of the program. I know you are so overqualified, but would you consider moving from temporary manager into being our permanent one? We're looking into an employee benefits package and hope to offer you more money soon."

Her eyes widened. "Seriously?"

"I wouldn't joke about this."

"I don't think you'd lie about anything. Can I think about it?"

That wasn't the answer he'd hoped to hear, but he realized Callie was a processor and needed to think through her decisions.

"To be honest, I didn't mean to spring this on you in my SUV. I meant to talk about it over the dinner we haven't had yet. Take all the time you need. We still have another month of summer, so let me know if I need to start looking again for someone else." Then Wyatt released his seat belt and shifted closer to her. "While you're considering that, there's something else I'd like you to consider."

"What's that?"

"Would you consider going out with a widower who has a super cute daughter?"

Callie laughed. "Well, that daughter sure is a strong draw."

Wyatt tapped her on the nose. "Sure, hang out with me for the sake of my kid."

Callie rested her cheek against his chest. "I think it's a package deal. And yes, I would love to. And you invited me to dinner already."

"I wasn't sure if you were still interested." Wyatt cradled Callie's face and brushed a kiss across her lips.

"Can I ask you something, Wyatt?"

"Sure thing."

"When I first came to town, you weren't ready to date."

"How do you know that?"

Callie's cheeks brightened again. "Your siblings may have mentioned it a time or two...or three."

"Of course. When you came into town, I wasn't interested."

"So, what changed?"

"You."

"I haven't changed."

Wyatt shook his head. "No, I mean being around you has changed me. You've given me hope." He nodded at the rearview mirror. "Remember that?"

She reached for the small stained glass dove like the one she found on her first day back at the shop. "I didn't even notice it hanging there. You found Gram's dove."

"After our conversation, I dug it out and decided to hang it where I would see it often. To remind me to hold on to hope." Wyatt buckled his seat belt in place.

He'd pulled back onto the road when his phone rang. Irene's number flashed on the screen. He accepted the call.

"Hey, Mama D. You're on speakerphone in my SUV. Callie's here. What's going on?"

She sniffed. "Wyatt, I'm so sorry to keep calling you. But it's Ray again."

Wyatt fingers tightened on the steering wheel. "What's going on?"

"He's having trouble breathing, so I called 911. They're on their way, but I have Mia."

"I'll be there in two minutes."

He ended the call and pressed down the gas. His fingers tightened on the steering wheel. "I'm sorry to ask this of you again, but would you mind watching Mia for me? You're welcome to take her to the lodge or to the ranch. I'll leave you my SUV and take Ray's truck to the hospital."

"Yes, of course. Promise you'll keep me posted?"

"Yes." He reached for her hand and squeezed. "Thank you, Callie. Once again, you're a lifesaver. In ways you'll never know."

Callie should've told Wyatt about the job opportunity in Colorado Springs when he offered her the full-time position at the guest ranch. But things were going so well and she didn't want to ruin anything.

Her conversation with Brian from that morning still played in her head. He'd told her about his gallery and his vision, and had outlined the job responsibilities. Then he'd dangled a very generous salary and benefits package that kind of took away her breath.

She did need a job with a little more money and benefits.

Then her talk with Wyatt on the way into town and now caring for Mia stirred up a lot of conflicted emotions.

She'd been in Aspen Ridge only a short time, but the little girl had already wriggled her way into Callie's heart.

How could she leave Wyatt and Mia?

Working at the guest ranch filled her heart with the peace and serenity she had been craving since receiving that phone call about her grandma's stroke.

The guest ranch was part of her healing journey, and she'd always appreciate that, no matter what she decided.

But what if it didn't work out with Wyatt? Would she have to leave Aspen Ridge?

While Mia played tag with the Herricks' granddaughters, Callie finished setting out items for the leaf printing she planned to do with Avery and Lexi, Wyatt's nieces, and the children visiting the guest ranch.

The Stone River Ranch truck pulled in next to Callie's car. Nora rounded the front, holding a floral arrangement, and headed toward Callie.

"Hey, Nora."

"Hi, Callie" She reached the table and set the arrangement in front of Callie. "These were just delivered to the ranch house, but they're for you."

"For me?" Callie fingered one of the satiny petals. Zinnias, hydrangeas and roses in different shades of pink and assorted ferns and greenery were arranged in a clear glass vase.

Callie pulled the small white card out of the bouquet and read it.

Please say yes.

Although there was no signature, the flowers had to have been from Brian, Jacie Brewster's brother, who wanted her to be the director for his art gallery.

Had this opportunity come a month or so ago, she might have been all over it.

But that was before Wyatt. And Mia.

"Thanks for bringing them by, Nora."

Nora sat on the picnic table bench next to Callie and slid an arm around her shoulders. "You're welcome. Thank you for everything you've done for my family, Callie. And I don't mean as manager of this place." She waved a hand over the property. "You've given my son something I haven't seen in a long time."

"What's that?"

"Hope."

Callie's fingers tightened around the envelope. Hope.

She nodded, then bit her bottom lip. "He did the same to me. I wasn't in a good place when I arrived in Aspen Ridge."

"We love having you here, you know."

Callie nodded. "Wyatt told me earlier. Thank you for that."

"Like my son, I'm not one to dig into other people's business, but I think you should know that Jacie Brewster's mom and I are good friends."

Callie's head jerked up. "So you know."

Nora nodded. "I know Brian offered you the gallery director position." She reached for Callie's arm. "And if that's where you feel God is leading you, then go with our blessing. But I ask that you talk with my son first, please. As his mother, I don't want to see him get his heart broken."

Callie swallowed against the lump in her throat and tried not to let Nora's words stir up guilt. "The last thing I want to do is hurt Wyatt. Or Mia. I'm crazy about both of them. That's the problem. The gallery director job would be great, but I'm not the same person I was a couple of months ago. And I have Gram's shop to consider."

"Your grandma would want you to follow God's leading as well, even if it meant selling and relocating."

"That's just it—I don't know where He's leading me. If it were up to me, I'd stay right here. But shouldn't I at least consider this other opportunity?"

"You're the only one who can answer that. Give it up to God, sweetie, and ask Him to align your heart with His will. That way, you won't go wrong with making the right choice. His plan for you is perfect, no matter if it's here in Aspen Ridge or in the Springs. Or even some other place in the world."

Callie reached over and hugged the woman. "Thanks, Nora. I appreciate you. Can we please keep this conversation between us?"

"Absolutely."

As Nora headed into the lodge, Callie rounded up the kids and directed them to the table. As she showed them how to press their ferns onto their paper and spray with the watered-down paint she'd mixed, Nora's advice tumbled over in her head.

She valued the loyalty of keeping her word, but the gallery promised financial security that she needed right now.

She had no idea what to do.

But she was going to figure it out somehow.

Chapter Thirteen

Wyatt pulled into the empty parking space by the lodge. The nightly campfire glowed down by the lake. Laughter drifted toward the treetops.

As he exited his SUV, he noticed Callie's light on in her suite. He headed into the lodge and took the stairs two at a time.

The door to her room was open about six inches, and he started to knock, but then he heard her talking. He took a step back, not wanting to interrupt.

Then she laughed. "Yes, Brian. The flowers did arrive. They're beautiful. I appreciate them." She paused, then spoke again. "The gallery director position would be perfect, but like I told Jacie, there's a lot to consider. I promise to have an answer for you soon."

Wyatt's heart slammed against his rib cage so hard he nearly winced in pain.

Was she talking to Brian Watkins? Didn't he have an art gallery in Colorado Springs?

At least that was what Aaron Brewster, Brian's

brother-in-law and the Stones' attorney, had told Wyatt when he ran into him at the diner a month or so ago. Aaron, Jacie and their son were heading to the Springs for a mini vacation to check out the new gallery.

No wonder Callie needed to think about accepting the full-time guest ranch management position.

If it weren't for Callie caring for Mia, Wyatt would've left without making his presence known. But he couldn't leave without his daughter.

Blowing out a breath, he braced the frame with one hand and rapped on the open door with the other.

Still on the phone, Callie opened it wider, and her eyes grew large. She waved him inside, then turned her back to him. "Listen, I have to go. I'll call you in a couple of days. Thank you. Bye."

Then she turned him. "Hi, Wyatt. How's Ray?"

"Daddy!" Mia scrambled off the little love seat where she had been coloring and ran over to him. She wrapped her arms around his legs. "Callie and I made a picture for you and one for Pappy too."

He took the papers she waved at him and barely glanced at them. "Thank you, sweetie."

As he lifted her in his arms and slung her backpack over his shoulder, he caught sight of the flowers on Callie's small table. A white card poked out of the colorful bouquet.

Please say yes.

Three little words that jammed a spike in his chest.

Callie reached for Ella the Elephant on the love seat and handed the stuffed animal to Wyatt. "Are you staying for the campfire?"

Was she really going to pretend he didn't over-hear her conversation?

He handed the elephant to his daughter. "No, I need to get Mia home. It's past her bedtime."

"Daddy, I wanna go back to the campfire." Mia rubbed her eye as she leaned against Wy-att's leg.

"Not tonight, honey. A different day."

One when Callie wouldn't be there.

"Are you still on for field volleyball tomor-row?" Callie folded her arms in front of her. "Cole and Bear set up the nets after dinner."

"I can't think about that now. My family needs me."

"How's Ray doing?" She rested a hand on his arm.

"He has pneumonia." Wyatt forced himself not to shake her hand off. He reached down and hooked Mia's sandals around his fingers.

"I'm sorry to hear that. Is there anything I can do?"

"You've done enough with looking after Mia. Thank you." Each word snapped like a bite, but he didn't care.

Callie's head shot up. "What's with the snappy tone?"

Wyatt dragged a hand over his face. Then he jerked his head toward the flowers. "Nice bouquet. Are you planning on taking the gallery director position? If so, at least give me a two weeks' notice so I can fill your position without burdening my family."

Callie's mouth opened, then closed again. "How much did you hear?"

Fatigue robbed him of his manners. "Enough. I have to get Mia home."

"Wyatt." She reached for him once again.

This time, he shook off her arm. "What about all that talk about reopening your grandmother's shop?"

"If you'd listen for two minutes, then I could tell you that I was offered the job, but I haven't made a decision yet. There are too many other things to factor in."

"When were you going to tell me? You must've had a good laugh at my full-time offer."

"That's not fair. And I'd never laugh at you." The hurt in her eyes had him softening his tone.

"What's not fair is that you couldn't trust me

with this information. When did you learn about the position?"

"A couple of days ago."

"A couple of days." He nodded, grinding his jaw.

"I planned to talk to you about it today, but then you got the call about Ray. I wasn't going to keep this from you. I just needed a little time to process everything."

"Well, don't let me keep you. I'll give you all the time you need. Thank you for caring for Mia." Wyatt all but slammed the door behind them.

He was such an idiot.

How could he have risked his heart with someone who planned to leave?

Wyatt didn't have to worry about sleeping through his alarm in the morning when he'd tossed and turned all night long. His conversation with Callie had played on a loop in his head until the sun peeked above the mountains.

He'd risked putting himself out there only to learn she might not stick around. They hadn't gone on a real date yet, and he definitely wasn't in love with her.

Like he'd told his family weeks ago—he didn't have time for romance. He needed to focus on his responsibilities, namely his daughter, the ranch, and now the horse rescue.

Then why did his heart feel like it had been squeezed out like an old sponge?

With his head throbbing and his eyes filled with grit, Wyatt headed to the kitchen and filled a to-go mug with black coffee.

"Come on, Mia. Let's go," he called to his daughter.

"Coming, Daddy. What are we doing today?" She skipped out of her room wearing pink polka dotted shorts and a pink shirt he'd laid out for her last night after her bath. Ella the Elephant was tucked in the crook of her arm.

"You're hanging out with Nana while Uncle Bear and I take the guests on a trail ride."

Mia clapped her hands and twirled in a circle. "Yay. Will I see Callie too?"

He shook his head. "Probably not. She's pretty busy."

Mia's face fell as her bottom lip popped out. "Okay."

He didn't have only himself to consider. He needed to protect his daughter from getting hurt too. If that meant keeping her away from Callie while she was still in Aspen Ridge, then that was what he needed to do.

Ten minutes later, he dropped Mia off at the ranch house, ignoring his mother's fussing about the circles under his eyes, and headed for the barn. He needed to tack up the horses and load them into the trailer.

Staying busy would keep his mind off last night's disaster.

As he came out of the tack room carrying Dante's saddle and pad, Bear rounded the corner with his horse Ranger's halter in his hand. He stopped and gave Wyatt the once-over. "Man, you look rough. Bad night?"

Wyatt pushed past him. "Something like that."

"Wanna talk about it?"

"Nope." Wyatt set Dante's saddle on the rack, then headed for his stall.

"Does this have anything to do with Callie?"

Wyatt rested his arm on the stall door, then glared at his brother. "What part of 'nope' confuses you?"

Bear strode over to him and crossed his arms over his chest. "Maybe the part that has me questioning if you're up for this ride today."

"I have to. The guests are expecting it."

"Yes, and they are expecting someone to keep them safe as well. If your focus isn't where it needs to be, then tell me now."

Shaking his head, Wyatt waved away his brother's words and unlatched the stall door. "Don't go all big brother on me. I've seen you do your fair share of moping before you and Piper got together."

"Right, and that's why I can tell that something's off with you."

"I said I was fine."

"Whatever, man. Just make sure your head's on straight."

Grabbing onto his harness, Wyatt led Dante out into the aisle and hooked him to the crossties. He dug through the grooming bucket and found the hoof pick. One by one, Wyatt lifted Dante's legs and picked the stones and debris out of his hooves. He dropped the pick in the bucket and grabbed the brush. He ran it across the stallion's coat, removing bits of straw.

An ache began to throb behind Wyatt's eyes. Still holding onto the brush, he rested his forehead against Dante's neck.

He needed just a minute.

But no matter how tired he was, he had a job to do, with no time to mess around.

Wyatt put away the grooming tools, then reached for Dante's saddle pad. He positioned it, then lifted the saddle on the horse's back. Once everything was cinched and secured, he slid the bridle in place, unclipped Dante and led the horse out to the trailer.

Bear followed and loaded Ranger. Working

together but silently, they loaded the other two tacked horses, then headed to the guest ranch.

Bear parked the ranch truck alongside the paddock. As Wyatt stepped out of the truck, Callie came out of the lodge. She spotted him and paused. Then she turned around and went back inside.

He didn't have the time, nor the inclination to go after her. He slid his sunglasses in place and adjusted his hat.

As he rounded the back of the trailer, Bear caught his arm. "Tell me now if you can't ride, and I'll get Dad to cover you."

Wyatt shook off his brother's arm. "I told you I'm fine."

"You better be because here come our riders now." Bear jerked his head toward the yurt closest to the road.

Clark and Francine, an older couple from Ohio, stepped onto the deck dressed in creased jeans, shined boots and matching black-and-white plaid Western-cut shirts with pearl snaps. Their cowboy hats appeared to be brand new.

"Morning." Clark tipped his hat, then clutched his shiny belt buckle.

Wyatt bit back a smile. "Good morning. Ready to ride?"

"Yes, sir."

"Good. Clark, you'll be riding Storm. Fran-

cine, you'll be riding Cheyenne. Both are gentle
Quarter horses who are used to our trail rides."

Clark rubbed his hands together. "Can't wait
to tell the boys back home about our ranching
adventures."

Francine hugged her husband's arm. "Don't
worry, Clark. I'll take plenty of pictures so you
can show them off."

Wyatt unlatched the trailer and led Cheyenne
out first. He held onto the horse's harness and
motioned for Francine to come toward them. "I'll
guide you with mounting Chey."

As he instructed each step, Francine listened
intently. She put her left foot in the stirrup and
started to swing her right leg over the horse's
back. The saddle shifted sideways. She let out a
scream as she lost her balance, pinwheeled backward and landed hard on the ground.

Cheyenne nickered and stepped back, flick-
ing her head.

Everything happened so quickly, yet it played
out in slow motion.

"Francine!" Clark knelt next to his wife. "Are
you hurt?"

Bear pushed past Wyatt and sent him a sear-
ing look. "I thought you tacked up the horses."

"I did." Wyatt fisted his hands.

"Not very well." Bear growled at him.

Several of the guests who had been eating

breakfast or hanging out on their decks rushed over to Francine.

Heat scorched his neck and face as he stared at the saddle still resting sideways on Cheyenne.

He'd been around horses all his life, and he'd never messed up like that. Not only had he put Francine in danger, but it wasn't safe for Cheyenne either. Macey would have his head if he hurt her horse.

Clark helped Francine to her feet.

Wyatt moved past him and touched her arm. "I'm so very sorry, Mrs. Masters. Are you hurt? Can I get you anything? I'll fix the saddle so you can still ride."

Francine rubbed her lower back, then held up a hand and shook her head. "No, thank you. I changed my mind about riding."

Her husband glared at him. "Me, too. Come on, dear. Let's head inside to get you some ice."

As Clark helped Francine back to their yurt, Wyatt ground his teeth.

Maybe they weren't the type to handle a trail ride anyway. But that was still no excuse for his negligence. The guest ranch's number one concern was guest safety, and he'd blown that.

Bear nearly shoved him out of the way as he attended to Cheyenne.

Wyatt dragged a hand over his face and strode toward the lodge. Inside, he headed for the kitchen and filled a glass with water. His hands shook as he downed the liquid and peered out the window at the lake.

The main door slammed open. Wyatt didn't need to turn to know his brother had followed him inside. Bear's heavy footsteps announced his presence.

Still holding the glass, Wyatt turned.

Bear thrust a hand toward the yurts. "What was that?"

"I messed up. I thought I tightened the cinch."

"You should've double-checked before she tried to get on. We always double-check before allowing riders on our horses. Now she's hurt."

Wyatt set the glass on the counter and pressed his back against the sink. He scrubbed both hands over his face, then dropped them at his sides. "I know. I feel terrible."

"And you should. I told you, man, if your head wasn't on straight then you needed to let me handle it."

"And I said I thought I was fine."

"Well, we saw just how fine you are. Whatever is going on between you and Callie, fix it. Ask her out or do whatever you need to make it right."

Wyatt ran a thumb and finger over his gritty eyes. "There's no point."

"Why not?"

"Brian Watkins offered her an art director position at his new gallery in the Springs."

"She's leaving?"

Wyatt shrugged and held up his hands.

"So, you don't even know if she's taking the job?"

Wyatt lifted his head. "No."

"Dude, step up and fight for her. Show her that you want her to stick around. That is what you want, isn't it?"

"Who am I to stand in her way if this is what she wants?"

"You're the guy who's in love with her."

"I never said I was in love with her."

"You don't have to say it. It's written all over your face. I haven't seen you like this since you were mooning over Linnea. Listen, I get it. I've been there. I know what it's like to lose someone close to you."

"My situation is different."

"How so?"

"Imagine if you lost Piper and had to raise Avery on your own. How would you feel?"

"I hope I never have to find out. And I'm sorry that you did. But Linnea is gone and you can't live in the past. Callie is here now. Fight for her, man. Have the life that you've always wanted." Bear turned on his heel and strode out of the lodge, slamming the door behind him.

Wyatt chewed on his brother's words.

Was he giving up without a fight? Would Callie consider staying if he shared how he truly felt? Was she even ready for another relationship? The only way he'd know was if he manned up and did as his brother suggested.

It was time to fight for the woman he loved.

Yes, loved. He'd finally admitted the truth. Now he needed to tell Callie how he felt and hoped she wanted to stay.

Callie should've made her presence known, but when her name was mentioned, she moved away from the steps as the brothers argued, unaware of how their voices carried through the open space.

She held her breath, waiting for Wyatt to agree with his brother. But his silence crumbled her heart.

He didn't care if she stayed or left?

She had hoped to make a home in Aspen Ridge, but how could she stay now? She'd end up running into Wyatt and Mia and be reminded constantly of what she'd lost. Again.

Maybe it was time to call Brian and accept the job. At least she hadn't fully unpacked, so moving wouldn't be too difficult. At least physically.

But there was the shop to consider. How could she go back on her word?

Was Nora right? Would it be okay to sell if that was what God was leading her to do?

Problem was, she didn't know. And that was part of her struggle.

Whatever she decided, it didn't need to happen this minute. She needed to get back outside and pretend she heard nothing. Pretend her heart wasn't shattered into a million pieces inside her chest. Pretend she wasn't humiliated by the chance she'd taken with Wyatt.

The door slammed a second time, then silence reigned. Callie gripped the banister and headed downstairs. She let out a deep breath, forced a smile in place and headed for the door.

She reached for the doorknob as her phone vibrated in her pocket.

She pulled it out, not recognizing the unidentified number scrolling across her screen, but she answered anyway. "Hello?"

"Hi, this is Susan Hurst, the coordinator of the Durango Local Artists Exhibition. I'm looking for Callie Morgan."

"This is she." Why would an art show coordinator be calling her?

"Callie, I am pleased to inform you that your entry is one of our top three finalists in the watercolor category."

Callie frowned. "My entry?"

"Yes, ma'am, the watercolor landscape entitled Hope."

"Oh, yes..." Callie's voice trailed off as ice slid through her veins.

"I know this is short notice, but our awards dinner is this weekend. If you'll confirm your email, then we'll share details with you. You're welcome to bring a significant other or guests, if you'd like. All we request is an RSVP within the next twenty-four hours."

Significant other? That certainly wouldn't be happening. And her family was too far away to make a last-minute trip.

She was on her own in a place she could no longer call home now.

Especially after what he'd done.

The call ended, and Callie clutched her phone. Her chest heaved as tears scalded her eyes.

She threw the door open so hard it smacked against the wall. She spied Wyatt heading to the ranch truck.

With her hands curled into fists and adrenaline rushing through her, she rushed across the grass, nearly running to catch him before he could get away.

Wyatt opened the truck door.

Chest heaving, she reached above him and slammed it shut. He whirled around. "Callie, what are you doing?"

"What am *I* doing? You have some nerve." She poked her phone into his chest.

His brows furrowed. "What are you talking about?"

She waved her phone in front of him. "I just got a call from the Durango Local Artists Exhibition. Apparently, my entry finaled in the top three."

His eyes widened, and then he smiled. "Hey, that's fantastic. Congratulations."

"You have got to be joking. It's not fantastic. You went behind my back and entered my piece after I specifically said it wasn't my best work. And now it's out there for everyone to see. How could you betray me like that?"

His mouth flopped open like a caught trout. He lifted his hands and then dropped them at his sides. He tucked his chin to his chest and shook his head. "I'm sorry."

"Sorry isn't good enough." She started to walk away, then turned back to him. Her vision blurred and a tear trickled down her cheek. "I heard your conversation with your brother. Even if you weren't too much of a chicken to ask me out, I'd say no now. I can't be with someone who I can't trust. Find yourself another manager because I'm done."

Callie had never walked off a job before, and

she truly hated leaving the Stones in the lurch right now, but there was no way she could stay.

To someone else, what Wyatt had done may not seem like that big of a deal. But after her experience with Shawn, she needed someone she could trust, even with the little things.

And Wyatt Stone had just proved he was not that man.

Chapter Fourteen

Wyatt wasn't about to let Callie walk away without hearing him out.

He looked at Bear. "Take over for me. I got to take care of this."

"Yeah, you do."

"Callie!" Wyatt jogged across the road and hurried to catch up to her.

She wrenched the door open. "I have nothing to say to you."

He followed her inside the lodge. "That's just fine. I have plenty to say. Now it's my turn to talk, and you need to listen to me."

"I don't need to do anything except leave."

"Callie, wait. Please." He hated the plea in his voice, but the weight of what had happened with the horse and now this just about did him in. He couldn't force her to listen but he hoped she would.

Her steps slowed. Even though she didn't turn around, she did stop. "What?"

He moved behind her and lifted a hand, then dropped it. If he touched her, he'd want to pull her into his arms, and that wouldn't solve anything. It would probably make matters worse.

He dragged a hand over his face. "I'm sorry. I truly am. I really loved the painting. You are so incredibly talented. You said your ex was dismissive of your talent. I just wanted to support your gift and show my appreciation."

She whirled around. Her reddened eyes shimmering with unshed tears sparked as she pounded the air with a clenched fist. "By going behind my back? You could've been more open and honest instead of being secretive. Now I have to deal with the fact that my art is out there. I confided in you and trusted you with the first thing I painted since losing my grandma. I even gave it to you as a gift, not to be put on display." Her voice broke as a tear slipped on her cheek.

He gentled his tone and took a step closer. "Callie, don't you see? That's what made the painting so beautiful. You brought the landscape to life with your vulnerability."

She shook her head. "It wasn't your decision to make. You should've been more open with me."

"You keep saying that, but you weren't being open with me. You didn't tell me about Brian's job offer."

"Because you got called away."

"You said you had known about it for a couple of days."

"And I was trying to process things so I could discuss it with you. But then with everything that happened with Ray, it wasn't the best time to talk about it."

"It's a great job, so I could see why you'd want to."

She dropped her chin to her chest, then lifted her head and looked at him, shaking her head. "If you think it's about the job, then you're an idiot, and you don't see anything at all. In fact, you're a hypocrite."

"What?" Wyatt scowled.

"You heard me. You stretch yourself so thin trying to keep everyone happy. You keep a mask in place so people don't see how you really feel. That's not being open and honest."

He flung his arms out. "People depend on me, Callie. I can't fall apart at every bad thing that happens."

"I get that, but when was the last time you allowed yourself to truly feel? When was the last time you were vulnerable, feeling like you were exposed for the whole world to see? Hmm?"

"I told you—the day my wife died. The day I realized I was twenty-five and had a newborn to care for. A newborn who would never know her mother. But I had to keep it together, I had to be strong for my daughter. Then I came home and found that my family's ranch was in trouble. My dad was sick. My siblings were going through their own struggles. They didn't need someone else to fall apart on them. I did what I had to. And if you can't understand that…"

She waved a finger in front of him. "I understand how you could go through a fog for so many months and come out and not remember much of anything. I understand how you can laugh and talk about a person in one breath, and then cry in the next. I understand the pain of losing someone you love. But I also understand that you have to allow yourself to work through those emotions so you can move toward healing. Have you done that, Wyatt? Because until you do, until you stop being strong for everyone else and allow yourself to have those moments of vulnerability, then there's no place for me in your life. I accept that you were married and will always love your wife. Now you have a beautiful daughter who does need you, but I also think that you haven't allowed yourself to fully grieve your heart-crushing loss." She looked up at him, tears coursing down her face. The brokenness in her eyes wrecked his chest.

Then she brushed the tears away with the back of her hand and reached in her pocket. She pulled out the keys he'd given her when she moved into the lodge. She pressed them into his hand and curled his fingers around the metal. "Goodbye, Wyatt."

She walked up the stairs to her suite while he remained rooted inside the door trying to breathe through the pain in his chest.

He'd fallen in love for the second time in his life. And for the second time, he'd lost that love.

Bear was right. Wyatt was a fool.

Callie had snuck out of the lodge like a coward, not even saying goodbye to Macey, Nora or any of the others who had been so kind to her.

Instead, she wrote a note and left it on the counter in the lodge kitchen. Hopefully they'd understand.

Leaving the lodge and the guest ranch…it shredded her. Even more so than when she had discovered that her ex-fiancé had a girlfriend.

At least she could crash in Gram's apartment until she figured out what to do next.

She dragged her suitcase up the steps and dropped it in the middle of the small living room. Then she reached for the knitted afghan, wrapped it around her shoulders even though it was about eighty degrees inside, and curled up on the love seat. She buried her face in the fibers and sobbed.

She had risked her heart only to have it broken again. Somehow, she needed to figure out how to put it back together.

Her phone rang, signaling a video call from her mother. Callie didn't want to talk, but she didn't want her mother to worry either.

She wiped her eyes with the back of her hand, but that didn't stop the tears from rolling down her face. She accepted the call. "Mom…"

"Callie, honey, what's going on? What's wrong?"

She could only shake her head until she regained her composure long enough to share what had happened with Wyatt.

"Oh, my sweet girl. I'm so sorry that you're hurting and I can't be there to comfort you."

"I don't know what to do, Mom."

"What's your heart telling you?"

Callie scoffed. "Are you kidding? My heart can't be trusted right now. I arrived at Stone River on what should've been my wedding day and fell for another guy who ended up betraying me. Even though he didn't cheat on me, he still went behind my back."

"Callie, I know what he did hurt you, and I'm not trying to diminish that. But, knowing Wyatt Stone as I do…well, as I used to when he was younger, I can't imagine that he did it with evil intentions. Sounds like he truly cares for you and wanted to show how much he believes in you."

"If he cared for me, then he should've been open and honest with me."

"You've said that several times, but what does that mean to you? He encouraged you to enter the show, and you told him no."

"It wasn't ready, Mom. I know you and Dad don't get my art, but it wasn't my best work."

"You shared your passion for art with your grandmother, but I do understand what it means to have a passion for something you love. Your dad and I gave up full-time careers in the States and moved away from our children to another part of the globe because God called us to minister to people in South America. Others might not understand that, but we did what we had to do. So, only you know your own heart. But you have to remember that your value isn't tied to your art or your family or even the shop. You are God's child, and He values you above all else. Do you still have Gram's letter?"

Callie nodded as her eyes drifted across the room to the small bookcase where she had set her letter. She hadn't been ready to read it when Aaron Brewster had given it to her, or even after she had returned to Aspen Ridge.

"Maybe you need to take time and read it."

They talked for a couple more minutes and then hung up, but not before Callie promised to call her mother again the next day.

She ran her fingers through the tangled mess of her hair and tossed her phone on the cushion. She stood and walked to the bookcase. She pulled out one of Gram's sketch journals and slid the letter out from between the pages.

Returning to the love seat, she pulled the knitted blanket over her legs and pressed the envelope to her nose. She inhaled the familiar scent that filled her mind with memories. Then she ran her finger under the seal and pulled out the envelope.

With trembling fingers, she unfolded the page and read.

Dear Callie,

I'm so blessed to have you as my granddaughter and grateful for every moment we spent together. I'm so thankful you shared my love of art, even if our family didn't quite get us.

I bought the blue cottage to give local artists an outlet for their creativity. Now I'm leaving it to you. It needs a bit of work, but I left a little money with Aaron for some of the repairs.

If it's a burden, or if God is calling you in a different direction, then I release you from your promise to reopen and give my bless-

ing to sell. It's all good as long as you're
following the Lord's leading.
Love and prayers,
Gram

Callie rested her head against the back of the
love seat as a trail of tears slid down her face.
She'd been released from her promise, but what
was God really calling her to do?

Maybe she needed to take time and listen to
her heart.

Chapter Fifteen

At least something was going right for someone.

Wyatt pulled his SUV up to the front door of Aspen Ridge General and shifted the engine into Park. He exited and rounded the front to open the passenger side as the nurse wheeled Ray outside.

"Good to see you, Ray. You look a lot better than you did the last time I saw you. Think you can try to stay out of hospitals for a while?"

"I feel it too." He maneuvered his crutches, thanked the nurse, then hauled himself into the passenger seat. "Sorry to pull you away to come get me, but they wanted to kick me out, and Irene was busy with handling an adoption at the animal shelter."

"Not a problem." Once Ray was secure, Wyatt shut the door and moved back behind the wheel. "Need to go to the pharmacy or any other place while we're out?"

Ray shook his head and patted the plastic bag on his lap. "Let's head home. Doc gave me enough meds until my prescriptions are ready. The pharmacy will deliver them later today. I just want to get home and rest. Can't sleep for anything in those hospitals."

"You got that right." Wyatt drove through the parking lot and headed back to Ray and Irene's.

"What's going on with you?"

Wyatt glanced at Ray while he waited for his turn at the intersection. "What are you talking about?"

"Not very chatty."

"And that's a bad thing?"

"Usually, you're asking me all sorts of questions. Now you've clammed up."

Wyatt kept his eyes on the road. "Sorry, don't feel like talking, I guess."

"Why not?"

Wyatt worked his jaw as he considered his next words. He opened his mouth and found himself spilling everything that happened in the past day or so with Callie.

"Pull over."

Wyatt jerked his eyes toward Ray. "You okay? Are you going to be sick?"

The older man scowled. "No, nothing like that. I want to talk some sense into you, and I don't wanna do it while you're driving. So, pull over."

Wyatt rolled his eyes at his father-in-law's

gruff tone, but he found a safe spot, pulled off the road and shifted into Park but left the engine idling.

Resting an arm over the steering wheel, he turned in his seat. "Okay, let me have it. You won't be the first, and I'm sure you won't be the last."

"Son, you are not responsible for making others happy, especially at the expense of your own mental health. You can't shut down how you feel for the sake of someone else. They are responsible for their own emotions and reactions. You're responsible for your own choices and your own actions."

"I have to be strong for my family."

"What does that even mean? You're one of the strongest young men I've known. Otherwise, I wouldn't have let you within ten feet of my daughter. I know Marines are tough and all that, but your strength doesn't lie in not showing your emotions. Your strength comes from who you are and how you use your faith to glorify God. It's not about denying yourself in order to keep others happy."

Wyatt puffed out his cheeks. "My faith isn't as strong as you think it is."

"What if it's not as weak as you think it is?"

Wyatt hadn't expected him to twist the question, and he didn't know how to respond.

"I'm a gruff cowboy. I was born in this town, and I'm going to die in this town. I don't travel much, and I'm fine with that. Everything I want is here. Except for more time with my daughter. But the Lord didn't see fit to give that to me. When I first injured my leg, I threw myself a big ole pity party. I shut Irene, Mia and you out because I didn't know how to express my own feelings. And for that, I'm sorry. This bout of pneumonia was a wake-up call. I'm done feeling sorry for myself. This cast is temporary, then I'll be back doing what I love."

Wyatt grinned. "I'm glad to hear that."

Ray lifted his chin. "I meant what I said. Guys have been taught for generations that emotions are signs of weakness. But you can mourn and be sad and still be strong. It's time to open your heart to your future, whatever that may be." Ray rubbed a hand across his whiskered chin. "Oh, and yeah, I'm taking back the horse rescue."

"What? Why would you do that?"

"I've been taking advantage of you lately, and that's got to stop."

"That's ridiculous. I'm family. You're not taking advantage of anything."

He raised an eyebrow and shot Wyatt with a direct look. "Okay, then. Maybe you're the one who's been taking advantage of me. You're saying yes and burying yourself in all kinds of work and projects. Now it's affecting other parts of your life. Maybe you're worried if you stop for any length of time, then you just might have to feel something."

"What's wrong with that?"

Ray rested a hand on Wyatt's shoulder and gave it a gentle squeeze. "If you don't move through your grief, then you can't heal the pain."

"Why does everyone keep saying that? I'm fine."

"Are you?"

"What do you want me to say, Ray?" Hot tears flooded Wyatt's eyes. To his horror, they leaked out and slid down the side of his nose. "Okay, maybe I'm not fine. Maybe I'm angry. What should've been one of the happiest days of my life is also one of the most heartbreaking. I lost my wife on the day I gained my daughter. I can't celebrate Mia without remembering what was taken from her. From me. And I'm angry at God for taking her. She was only twenty-four-years old. Why did she have to die?"

Ray's chin trembled as he swallowed several times. "I don't have an answer because I've asked that question many times. I had to learn to stop asking God why and instead ask Him what He wants me to learn through this. Irene reminds me that God allows things to happen so He can write our stories the way they need to be told." He ran a hand under his nose. "Look at what you've done since you've moved back to Aspen Ridge. For the last three years, you've guided a group of men into learning how to become strong single fathers. You couldn't have done that without losing your wife."

Wyatt dried his eyes with the heel of his hands. "I'd rather have my wife."

"I'd rather have my daughter too, but that wasn't God's plan. And it's okay to be mad at God. He can handle it. The more you allow Him to work in your life and through your grief, the more He can use you to tell the next part of your story."

Wyatt rested his head against the seat and closed his eyes. "How did you and Irene do it? How did you move through your grief?"

Ray sighed. "Not very well at first. For the first month after Linnea died, Irene refused to get out of bed until Ada paid her a visit and said Linnea wouldn't want her to live like that. Ada reminded her what it meant to hold on to hope. And that our time on earth was only temporary compared to eternity in Heaven. And I think knowing that she would see her little girl someday motivated Irene to live a life that honored her daughter here on earth. We will always miss our daughter until we're reunited in Heaven. We sought counseling and attended a grief support group at church. We keep Linnea's memory alive by sharing stories. We had to learn how to live a new kind of normal without her, but we are overjoyed to have Mia and you."

"Ada Morgan was quite a lady."

"Yes, she was. And so is her granddaughter."

Wyatt held up a hand. "Don't even go there."

"Why not?"

"Because things between Callie and me are over before they could really get started."

"Only if you let it, son."

"Callie made it clear she wants nothing to do with me. I'm sure she'll be leaving Aspen Ridge soon, anyway."

"Then change her mind. Fight for her. Show her that you're the kind of man she needs in her life. Because I'm telling you right now, she's the kind of woman you need, and she'll make an exceptional mother for Mia. I've watched the two of them together. Mia adores her too."

Wyatt nodded. "Yes, and that's what worries me. Mia getting attached and then getting her heart broken."

"If that happens, she'll survive because Mia is strong like her daddy and has her mother's blood in her. But this doesn't have to be the end of the story for you and Callie. You have to decide where you want to go from here—live in the past or fight for your future."

With his father-in-law's words echoing inside his head, Wyatt turned back to the steering wheel and shifted the engine into Drive as he headed back to Ray's ranch.

Was Ray right? Only one way to find out.

Now, if only he could get Callie to give him a second chance…

Last minute was better than not at all.

Callie didn't want to attend the awards reception, but Gram's comment in her letter about pursuing her passion sparked Callie to RSVP for a party of one.

Maybe that was part of the problem—she didn't want to show up alone.

Truth was, she missed the guest ranch. She missed Mia. But most of all, she missed Wyatt.

For the past couple of days, she'd waffled about how to approach him, how to apologize for her outburst. Now that she had time to think about it, she saw the tenderness behind his intentions. He believed in her, believed in her talent in a way that no one else other than Gram ever had. He wanted only the best for her.

But her best didn't come with awards or ribbons. Her best came from being around him. And she'd blown it.

So she planned to show up, accept her ribbon and leave.

Simple as that.

The reception invitation hadn't specified a dress code. How did one dress for an art exhibition?

Callie hoped her three-quarter-sleeved coral wrap dress with the geometric design and taupe slingback sandals were enough. She'd twisted her hair into a French knot and secured it with a couple of Gram's combs. She'd also found an ivory beaded handbag in Gram's closet.

She headed inside the gallery and gave her name at the reception table. The tall woman behind the table was dressed in a black-and-white striped cocktail dress with hot pink pumps.

She handed Callie a program, a name tag, and her table number.

She didn't plan on staying long enough to eat, but the program showed that dinner would be served first, then the awards ceremony. She had to sit at a table with a bunch of strangers. Or worse yet—by herself. Her only other option was to leave. That was tempting.

She bypassed a waiter carrying a tray of appetizers and entered the gallery where different art pieces sat on display. Tucking her handbag under her arm, she perused the pen-and-ink drawings, acrylics, oils and, finally, the watercolors.

On the back wall, three framed watercolors hung in a row under spotlights hanging from the ceiling. Callie stood in front of her painting and tried to see what Wyatt saw.

She had gotten up early that first morning after arriving at the guest ranch and taken a walk. Sunlight hovered over the horizon and cast the glow across the lake. In the distance, the ranch house sat quietly nestled against the mountains. The image had taken her breath away and she couldn't wait to capture it with color. She had taken a picture with her phone, but it didn't do it justice.

And neither did her painting.

As she stepped closer, she realized a ribbon hung from the bottom of the frame. She turned it around and gasped.

She had taken first place.

She couldn't believe it. And there was no one to celebrate with.

"Beautiful workmanship." A deep, male voice spoke behind her.

That voice sounded too familiar...

Callie turned discreetly and tried to look over her shoulder without appearing obvious.

Then she gasped out loud.

"Dad!" She threw her arms around the older man standing behind her as tears clouded her vision. "What are you doing here?"

He gripped her arms, then kissed her forehead. "I've never missed an art show, and I wasn't about to start now."

Callie rested her cheek against his chest, not caring if it messed up her updo, and wrapped her arms around his waist. "I'm so glad you're here."

Dad wrapped his arms around her and then turned her toward her table. "Not just me. Your mom and brothers are here too."

Callie peered around him. "Are you serious?"

"Absolutely. After your mom hung up with you the other day, she called me and we booked tickets. We've decided to take a short break but we'll be here for as long as you need us."

"But what about your ministry?"

"We left it in good hands. They understand family emergencies, especially when we said our daughter needed us."

Callie bit her bottom lip, trying to hold back the emotion that filled her chest. "Thank you, Dad."

"No thanks necessary, sweetheart. I wish you had been more up-front about some of the struggles you've been facing."

Callie shrugged. "Can't run to my daddy every time there's a problem."

Her father lifted her chin and looked her squarely in the eye. "Actually, that's exactly what you're supposed to do. Your Heavenly Father wants to know about every struggle. Even if I can't be here, He is always here with you."

"Thanks for the reminder. Too often, I think I need to handle things on my own."

"How's that working out for you?"

"These days, not very well."

They reached the table where Callie thought she'd be sitting alone. Instead, her mother sat with Wesley and Trevor. Callie flew into her mother's arms, having not seen her since a week after Gram's funeral. Although, she appreciated the face-to-face connection, video chatting just wasn't the same. Then she hugged her brothers. "I can't believe you guys are here."

Then she noticed three other chairs had been taken. Maybe the committee had put them with another family.

Sitting next to her mom, Callie felt more settled than she had since her blowup with Wyatt. In the middle of talking about her most recent project in Chile, Mom paused and looked above Callie's head.

Callie turned to see what had caught her mother's attention, and her breath caught for like the hundredth time that day.

She stood slowly. "Wyatt, what are you doing here?"

Wyatt stood behind her, dressed in charcoal-colored dress pants and a light blue button-down shirt with sleeves rolled up, revealing his tanned forearms. He held his cowboy hat in his hand, running his fingers around the brim.

"Congratulations, Callie. I saw your painting had taken first place. I knew it was a winner from the moment I saw it, no matter what the judges had decided. But I see they saw the same value in your talent as I did."

"Thank you."

He took her hand, running a thumb over her knuckles, and gave her fingers a gentle squeeze. He looked at her with pleading in his beautiful blue eyes. "Please hear me when I say how sorry I am for going behind your back."

She looked down at his strong hands and long fingers. Hands that worked hard, tamed horses and wiped his daughter's tears. Then she lifted her gaze to meet his eyes and she smiled. "Thank you, Wyatt. I appreciate that. Now it's my turn."

He frowned. "Turn for what?"

"To apologize. After I left the guest ranch without giving you notice, I realized your motives weren't to betray me but to support me and my passion. I couldn't see past my own insecurities, and I overreacted. I'm sorry for what I said and for walking away."

He shook his head. "I shouldn't have entered your piece without your consent. You asked me to be more honest with what I'm feeling. I'll do that now. I love you, Callie. I will protect you, fight for you, and trust you every day. More than anything, I'd love for you to stay in Aspen Ridge. I'll help you get Ada's shop restored and reopened, and you can help me run the horse rescue. We'll be busy all the time, and you may have regrets, but we can face them together. However, if you want to take the art director position at the gallery, then I hope you wouldn't mind if a weary cowboy and his adorable daughter joined you."

"You'd do that—give up your dreams—for me?"

"If it means we'll be together, then yes."

"There's something I need to tell you."

"What's that?"

Smiling, she cupped his cheek. "I won't be taking the job at the gallery. I'm not leaving Aspen Ridge."

"What made you change your mind?"

"Well, I hadn't actually made up my mind to take it. I had to consider everything I was giving up, and it wasn't worth the cost."

"Your gram's shop?"

She shook her head. "I've been released from that promise. I love Gram's cottage, and it will always hold wonderful memories. I was referring to you. And Mia. I can't move away from the man I love. Or his adorable little girl."

Wyatt cradled her face in his hands. He

brushed a kiss across her lips. Then he gathered her in his embrace. "I've missed you. It's only been two days but it feels like it's been two weeks."

"Get used to having me around, because I'm not going anywhere."

He kissed her again. "I like the sound of that."

Epilogue

Had it been only nine months since she'd returned to Aspen Ridge, ready to keep her promise to her grandma? Nine months since Wyatt had rescued her from the side of the road? Nine months since her planned life had taken an unexpected turn?

And now, nine months later, she was about to walk down the aisle to exchange vows with the man who'd helped her to hold on to hope.

Callie stood in front of the full-length mirror in her former suite at the lodge. She ran her hands over the V-neck lace gown with the beaded appliques at the shoulders and a sweeping train. Her hair had been twisted in a low knot at the base of her head. She'd secured the midlength veil with the jeweled combs that Gram had worn on her own wedding day so many years ago.

Macey, Everly and Mallory had gone into one of the other nearby suites to get ready so Callie had a few minutes to herself before the wedding ceremony began.

When Wyatt had proposed at Thanksgiving, letting her know how grateful he was to her for showing up in his life, they decided they didn't want a long engagement. No matter how clichéd it was, they'd chosen February to pledge their love. Since they came together because of the guest ranch, Callie wanted to have a small ceremony there with only family and close friends in attendance. Wyatt was more than happy to give her what she wanted.

Just then, someone knocked on her door.

"Come in."

Irene peeked inside. "Mind if I come in a minute?"

Callie turned away from the mirror and waved her in. "Not at all."

Irene stepped into the room, looking gorgeous in an emerald green dress, and brought her hand to her mouth. "You look beautiful. Wyatt won't be able to focus on what Pastor Miles is saying. He'll have eyes only for you."

"Thank you, Irene." Callie pressed a hand against her stomach. "I don't know why I'm so nervous. I have no doubts about marrying Wyatt and being a mother to Mia."

"Every bride is nervous on her wedding day. It's normal. But the moment you see Wyatt, those nerves will disappear. I brought you something." She reached into her purse and pulled out a white velvet pouch. She withdrew a delicate silver bracelet and laid it across the palm of her hand. "Your grandma gave this to me on the first birthday I celebrated without my daughter. Linnea wore Ada's pearls on her wedding day, so I thought I would offer this and see if you'd like to wear it."

Callie smiled as she ran her finger over the charm of a dove holding a heart in its mouth with the word *HOPE* engraved on it. She looked at Irene and smiled. "It's beautiful. I'd be honored to wear it. Thank you for thinking of me."

She held out her wrist, and Irene fastened the bracelet. She kissed Callie's cheek, then pulled her in for a hug. "Absolutely, my dear. Ray and I are so pleased with how you and Wyatt have come together. We couldn't have asked for a more special person to be a part of his and Mia's lives."

"I'm the one who's blessed. I'm excited to start our lives together as a family."

Irene hugged her again. "I'll scoot out of here so you can finish getting ready."

When the door closed, Callie sat on the end of the bed and slid her feet into the beaded ballet slippers. The fourteen-year-old girl inside her couldn't believe she was about to walk down the aisle any minute and marry Wyatt Stone.

A knock sounded on her door again. This time, Callie stood and opened it.

Her father stood in the doorway looking handsome in his dark gray suit. "Callista, you look beautiful."

Callie glanced down at her gown, then back at him. "Thanks, Dad."

"You ready?"

She nodded and grabbed her bouquet of roses, miniature carnations and ranunculus in shades of navy, pink and blush.

As she stepped out of the room and closed the door behind her, Mia, dressed in her dusty pink flower girl dress, ran over to her and stopped. Her eyes grew wide "You look like a princess, Callie."

Callie leaned over and kissed Mia. "Thank you. I feel like a princess. You look beautiful."

Mia twirled. "Thank you."

The music changed, and Macey herded everyone into position. Macey, Mallory, Everly and Piper, all wearing gowns in shades of blue, descended the stairs ahead of her, then Tanner walked with Mia as she tossed rose petals on the blush-pink runner.

Callie took a step down and caught Wyatt's eyes on her. Her knees nearly buckled at the sight of him standing in front of the stone fireplace in his gray suit with Bear, Cole, Trevor and Wesley next to him.

For the next ten minutes she listened to Pastor Miles talk about God's love and hope.

"The bride and groom have chosen to write their own vows." Pastor Miles nodded to Callie.

"Wyatt, when you saved me from the side of the road last June, I didn't realize how much my life would change. You are the kindest, most generous man I've known. I don't doubt your love or your support of what I do. I look forward to a lifetime of trusting you to keep my secrets, drying my tears, laughing and raising our family together. I give you my heart and all my love." She slid the band on Wyatt's finger and squeezed his hands.

"Callie, I accept the responsibility that comes with accepting the gift of your heart and love. I promise to love, protect, cherish and support you every day that we are given to be together. I'm truly blessed to have been given a second chance at happiness, and I'll never take it for granted." Wyatt paused a moment then looked at her lovingly. "You showed me what it means to be strong and how to continually hold on to hope. Through all the ups and downs that we'll face, I'm so thankful we'll face them together as partners and as friends. My love for you grows daily, and I'm excited to begin our life together as a family." Wyatt's voice caught on the last word as his eyes sparkled. He slid the ring on her finger, then lifted her hand and pressed his lips against her knuckles.

A tear slid down Callie's cheek, and Wyatt brushed it away gently with his finger as Pastor Miles blessed their union. Then he looked at Wyatt, "You may kiss the bride."

"About time." Wyatt wrapped an arm around Callie's waist and drew her against him. Then he kissed her.

Family and friends clapped, and gathered around them to share their congratulations.

For the next couple of hours, they ate, danced and laughed with the people they loved.

Callie sat on the arm of one of the couches, talking with Jacie. Wyatt rested his hands on her shoulders and whispered by her ear. "Can I steal you away for a moment?"

She turned to him. "Of course." After excusing herself away from Jacie, Callie took Wyatt's hand as he led her to the family table where Deacon and Nora sat.

As they approached, Deacon and Nora stood. Deacon retrieved an envelope from his inside suit pocket and held it out to them. "Wyatt and Callie, we are so thankful God has given both of you a second chance for happiness as Wyatt said in his vows. We love you both, and we are excited to see how God uses you. Hopefully, this will help."

Wyatt pulled out a letter and what appeared to be a check from the envelope. He wrapped an arm around Callie's waist, and they read it together.

Callie looked at Wyatt, then at her new in-laws. "Are you serious?"

"We don't mess around when it comes to our children's futures."

Wyatt looked at his parents. "I don't know what to say except thank you."

"That's all you need to say. When your brother and sister got married, they each received portions of Stone River. As the letter states, we are giving you the cabin and the land around it, but your share of the land is smaller. Now that Ray and Irene have given you the horse rescue, which you've turned into the sanctuary, we know how much that means to you. We decided partnering with Linnea's Hope is a better investment."

Wyatt blinked several times and swallowed hard. "Thank you. It's perfect."

Nora looked at them. "We are so proud of the both of you and know God has great things in store for your shop too, Callie."

After exchanging more hugs, Nora pulled a protesting Deacon onto the dance floor.

Callie turned to Wyatt and framed his face with her hands. "I love you, Mr. Stone."

His arms slid around her waist. "And I love you, Mrs. Stone. For the rest of my life."

"Hey, what about me?"

Callie and Wyatt broke apart to find Mia tugging on Wyatt's pant leg with Ella in her arms.

Wyatt lifted her in his arms. "What about you?"

Mia wrapped an arm around Wyatt and one around Callie. "I want to be a part of the hug."

Wyatt laughed and shifted her between them. "You're always a part of our hugs, Peanut."

Mia rested her head on Callie's shoulder. "I love you, Callie."

"I love you too, sweetheart."

"Lexi said when her daddy married Aunt Macey, she could call her Mommy. You married my daddy. Can I call you Mommy?"

Callie bit her lip and nodded. "I would love that, sweet girl."

Nine months ago, she'd arrived at Stone River brokenhearted, with her life in shambles.

But two people with no desire to fall in love again had held on to hope and come together to create their own happily-ever-after.

And she couldn't be more excited to build a life in Aspen Ridge with her handsome cowboy and his daughter.

* * * * *

Dear Reader,

I didn't want to write this story. When I plotted out this series, I knew Wyatt was going to be a single father who'd lost his wife. Originally, I had a different heroine, but she didn't seem to be the right fit, so I created Callie, who was also grieving after losing her grandmother.

You see—what I didn't expect was to be walking through my own grief journey. My mom was diagnosed with stage 4 cancer, and within four months, she passed away into the arms of Jesus.

I wrote Wyatt and Callie's story while mourning the loss of an amazing woman of God. I cried as I wrote the rough draft. I cried as I polished the novel. I cried as I submitted the story to my wonderful editor. I learned those tears were necessary and healing as was writing this story.

Grief is messy. And ugly. Riding those waves of emotions and memories can be exhausting. But grief also evolves. Even though my family misses my mom terribly, we are so thankful she is completely healed. We will see her again someday.

Through it all, God remains so good. No matter what season we are walking through, He sees our pain and captures our tears. Lean into Him and trust Him with all of it.

I hope you enjoyed Wyatt and Callie's story as they walked through their grief to embrace hope. May you hold on to hope and know God is with you every step of the way.

Blessings,
Lisa Jordan

HARLEQUIN
Reader Service

Enjoyed your book?

Try the perfect subscription for Romance readers and get more great books like this delivered right to your door.

See why over 10+ million readers have tried Harlequin Reader Service.

Start with a Free Welcome Collection with free books and a gift—valued over $20.

Choose any series in print or ebook. See website for details and order today:

TryReaderService.com/subscriptions

RSBPA24R